Also by Carolyn Brown

What Happens in Texas
A Heap of Texas Trouble
Christmas at Home
Secrets in the Sand
Holidays on the Ranch

Lucky Cowboys
Lucky in Love
One Lucky Cowboy
Getting Lucky
Talk Cowboy to Me

Honky Tonk
I Love This Bar
Hell, Yeah
My Give a Damn's Busted
Honky Tonk Christmas

Spikes & Spurs
Love Drunk Cowboy
Red's Hot Cowboy
Darn Good Cowboy Christmas
One Hot Cowboy Wedding
Mistletoe Cowboy
Just a Cowboy and His Baby
Cowboy Seeks Bride

Cowboys & Brides
Billion Dollar Cowboy
The Cowboy's Christmas Baby
The Cowboy's Mail Order Bride
How to Marry a Cowboy

Burnt Boot, Texas
Cowboy Boots for Christmas
The Trouble with Texas Cowboys
One Texas Cowboy Too Many
A Cowboy Christmas Miracle

Bride
for a
Day

CAROLYN
BROWN

sourcebooks
casablanca

Published by Sourcebooks Casablanca, an imprint of Sourcebooks
P.O. Box 4410, Naperville, Illinois 60567-4410
(630) 961-3900
sourcebooks.com

Originally published as *Love Is the Answer* in 1997 in the United States of America
by Precious Gem Romance, an imprint of Zebra Books. This edition based on the
paperback edition self-published by the author in 2014 as *Bride for a Day*.

Printed and bound in Canada.
MBP 10 9 8 7 6 5 4 3 2 1

Dear Readers,

In 1997, I started my writing career with four contemporary romance books written under the name Abby Gray. Writing was going to be my vice, and no one was going to know about it, but alas, my sister was so happy I was finally published that she put articles and congratulatory ads in three newspapers, and everyone found out.

Sourcebooks has given me the opportunity to bring those four books up to date. The story line is the same, but major changes have been made. This is one of those books that started out in 1997 as *Love Is the Answer*, then went to *Bride for a Day* when I reissued it about five years ago. The title is staying the same, but the cover and content have changed. I hope you all enjoy this brand-new edition with Cassie and Ted's story.

Twenty-four years and more than a hundred books after I got that first call back in 1997, I still have a special place in my heart for all my characters, but *Bride for a Day* is extra special because it's one of those first four books that kick-started my career in writing romance.

Like the old saying about it taking a village to raise a child, it takes more than just writing or rewriting a book to put a finished product in your hands. I'd like to thank all those who helped make this edition of *Bride for a Day* possible, starting with Sourcebooks and Deb Werksman for giving me the opportunity to rewrite the story. Then to my agent, Erin Niumata, and Folio Management for everything they do for my career. To my husband, Charles Brown, who doesn't mind eating take-out one more night so I can finish another chapter. And most of all to my amazing readers. You all are and will always be important to me.

Until next time,
Carolyn Brown

Chapter 1

CASSIE FROWNED AT HER REFLECTION IN THE CRACKED mirror above the lavatory in the women's restroom. She wanted to blend in with the folks in the convenience store and café combination, but since she was almost six feet tall and had red hair, that was nearly impossible.

"I need a scarf or a hat to cover up this telltale red hair." She pulled a brush through the tangled red curls that framed her oval face. "I should just slap a sign on my backpack that says *Return Me to Cecil Gorman*." She pulled her hair up into a ponytail, wrapped a rubber band around it twice, and hoped it was time for the bus to leave. She only had to walk down one aisle, past half a dozen booths, and out the door without running into the two policemen who had come into the place right after the passengers all piled off the bus.

In a few minutes, folks would begin to reboard the bus. In less than an hour, she'd be across the Texas state line and into Oklahoma. Not that it mattered which state she was in if Cecil wanted to come looking for her. When Deana died, he had told Cassie she had a choice—she could either get out of his house or do what he told her. She had no money and had taken care of Deana, his wife, for two years. She had no place to go. Her mother had died before her sixteenth birthday. She had no job because Cecil had insisted she give up her college scholarship and take care of Deana when she got lung cancer.

What Cecil told her meant she was being sold to a man who ran a sex trafficking ring out of Houston. He must have thought he gave her no way out, but she had taken the wedding rings her grandmother had left to her, pawned them, and bought a bus ticket to Oklahoma City. That was as far as she could get away from Cecil on the amount of money the pawnbroker gave her.

If the authorities said she had to go back to Cecil's place out in West Texas, they could just put her body in a pine box because she would never go back, not if she was still breathing. Her life would end right there in Lindsay, Texas, at a convenience store at the age of twenty. She would rather be dead than sold into the sex trafficking ring that Cecil had already gotten half payment for. She just needed a place to hide out for a little while. Hopefully, he would get tired of looking for her, and she would never see him again.

"Send me some luck, Mama," she whispered. "I don't even mind living in a trailer again. Living there was better than living in that house with Cecil anyway."

He was a long-haul truck driver, and things weren't so bad when he was out on the road for a week or more at a time. But when he came home for a day or two, everything was tense and even Deana acted different. Those days, except for cooking, cleaning, and taking care of the outside animals, she stayed in her tiny room.

Cassie couldn't stay in the bathroom another minute if she planned to reboard the bus. She took a deep breath and looked at her reflection in the dirty mirror one more time. "I look like you, Mama," she whispered.

Her mother had worked as a waitress at a diner out in the middle of nowhere in a little community called Maryneal. She brought home enough money to pay the bills, and Cassie had grumbled about having to ride the bus twenty miles morning and evening to the nearest high school.

"I'm sorry, Mama." Cassie wiped a tear from her mossy-green

eyes with the back of her hand. "If I knew then what I do now," she muttered, "I would never have said a word."

Her mother must have known something wasn't right a few weeks before the aneurysm burst in her head because she'd handwritten a will, leaving her few meager possessions to her daughter including the wedding rings that Cassie had pawned for money. There was a personal letter to Cassie telling her that in the event of her mother's death, arrangements had been made for her to live with the other waitress, Deana, and her husband, Cecil.

Everything changed in Cassie's life after that.

"I miss you so much," Cassie said. "Send down a miracle and help me stay away from Cecil for a few months, just until I can claim my inheritance, and if possible, could you help me find a job when I get to Oklahoma City? If you were here, you'd shoot him yourself for selling me like I was nothing more than one of Deana's goats."

The heavy rock that she seemed to carry in her heart from the day that she and Deana scattered her mother's ashes got even bigger two days after she had graduated from high school. That was the day they found out Deana had terminal cancer. Cecil laid a heavy guilt trip on Cassie.

"You've studied that nurses' aide stuff at the vo-tech these past two years, and you owe us for taking you in so that you didn't have to go to foster care in some gawd-awful place. You can pay us back by taking care of Deana while I'm out on the road making a living to put food in your mouth and pay the bills to keep a roof over your head," he had said.

"But I'm enrolled in college this fall. I've got a full scholarship to finish studying to be a nurse." She remembered tears flowing down her cheeks.

"You owe us, girl," Cecil had growled. "And besides, you are still just seventeen. I can call Social Services and turn you over to them. You want to go to foster care?"

"Please," Deana had begged. "I don't want someone I don't know coming in here to take care of me."

Cassie couldn't say no to Deana, but she'd cried herself to sleep for a week, and when college started that fall, she had cried for another week. Last week Deana had lost the battle with cancer, and Cecil came home to have her cremated. Cassie hoped that she might start to college as soon as the spring semester began, but the lady she talked to at the school said she would have to wait until fall when the new classes for nursing began.

"Last night was awful, Mama." Cassie sighed and turned away from the mirror. "First he tried to force me into bed with him, and then he went into a rage when I fought him off. This morning he told me that he'd sold me to a man who runs a little sex trade. I had no money, so I had to hock Granny's wedding rings. Why am I talking to you? You can't help me."

We always talk about everything, her mother's voice whispered in her ear.

Cassie took a deep breath, opened the bathroom door, and locked gazes with a uniformed policeman. He nudged the second one on the shoulder and nodded toward Cassie. They split up, but she could easily see they were trying to box her in. Her heart skipped two beats, fluttered a couple of times, then began to race. A fine sweat formed on her upper lip. The aroma of fried chicken wafted over to her, and her stomach growled. She'd love to walk right over to the deli and buy even just one chicken strip, but she couldn't afford to spend her last few dollars on food.

She imagined the chill of the handcuffs around her wrists. She scanned the diner connected to the bus stop, but the exit door was on the other side of the policemen, who had not taken their eyes off her.

She considered dashing back into the restroom and crawling out a window, but the only one in there was right up next to the ceiling. Evidently, her mother didn't have a lot of power in heaven because she hadn't provided a miracle or sent any help.

Those who help themselves get help. Her mother's words came to her mind.

That's when Cassie saw a young man sitting alone in one of the booths. She smiled and waved when she caught his eye. Pretending she didn't know there were two policemen between her and freedom, she forced her jelly-filled knees to carry her around the ends of the display shelves, past the potato chips that really looked good, and over to where he was sitting.

She slid into the booth across from the cowboy and watched the bus pull away from the curb. The time had come to swim or drown, and she'd come too far now to have to throw in the towel. Hopefully, this man wasn't a serial killer, or married, or both—or worse yet, someone Cecil had sent to find her.

=====

Ted Wellman had seen the redheaded woman when she came into the store with the rest of the folks who had gotten off the bus. She was a striking woman who carried herself like a runway model. He'd wondered why someone as beautiful as she was would take a bus rather than a plane. For several minutes after she disappeared into the ladies' restroom, he tried to figure out what television show or movie he had seen her on, and finally came up with an answer. She'd been on a couple of episodes of *Chuck*, a series that he and his brother, John, had watched several times. A closer look her way told him that she wasn't the character, Carina, so he went back to watching the people through the plate-glass window as he drank his coffee.

Then she came out of the restroom, locked eyes with him, and acted as if she knew him. Whoever she was, she was going to be embarrassed when she found out he didn't have the first idea who she was or where he'd seen her before.

"Hi, honey," she said, loudly enough for the two policemen behind her to hear. She reached across the table and laid a hand on his. "Please help me," she whispered. "Please say I'm with you."

Her green eyes looked desperate, even though a fake smile was plastered on her face.

Ted wasn't sure what to do. Could this be one of those television shows where they videotaped practical jokes on unsuspecting people? He just wanted to finish his coffee, get in his trusty old truck, and go back across the Red River to

Ryan, Oklahoma. He damn sure wasn't the right person for anyone to be playing a joke on.

"Please," she whispered again as the two policemen zeroed in on him and started toward them. "I just need a little help for a few minutes."

"Excuse me," the older policeman drawled. "Could I have a word with you?"

"Sure," Ted answered. "What's the problem, sir?"

"I'm Sheriff Bud Tucker and this is my deputy, Tommy Stevens. Who are you, gal?" He turned his focus toward the woman.

"Why do you want to know?" Ted asked.

The woman squeezed his hand and looked like any minute she would burst into tears. Ted flashed a smile her way and thought of his brother, John. There was no question in his mind that John would have helped this woman—no matter what she had done to bring the cops sniffing around. John had always been the daredevil twin, and that had gotten him killed a few years ago. For some reason, Ted thought of those bracelets that were still around. WWJD stood for What Would Jesus Do, but he always thought of the letters standing for What Would John Do. Ted and John were insep-arable, looked so much alike their mother could hardly tell them apart, and part of Ted's heart died the day his brother was killed.

WWJD? the pesky voice in his head asked.

Ted didn't even have to think about it. He knew what John would do.

Bud, the sheriff, had turned back to Ted. "Well?" he demanded.

"I'm sorry. What was the question?" Ted asked.

"Who is this woman?" Bud asked. "We were told to be on the lookout for a runaway from San Antonio. A woman that burglarized her benefactors' home and took things that don't belong to her, plus she's got some mental problems. Her name is Cassie Stewart and her uncle, Cecil Gorman, the man she has stolen from, has filed a missing person's report. According to him, she is tall, has red hair and green eyes, and is possibly headed north. He is looking for a picture of her to put with the report. It should come up on our computers anytime now."

Ted shook his head and said the first thing that came to his mind. "Sorry, guys. This is my girlfriend. We drove down here from Ryan, Oklahoma. Actually, we spent last night in Waco where we picked up some oil-well parts for my dad."

The sheriff drew his eyebrows down and crossed his arms

over his chest. "Oh, really! Something tells me that you're lying to me, son."

"No, sir. Cassie is my girlfriend, and"—he searched for something believable—"and we're going to get married today."

Good Lord, Brother, you didn't have to go that far! John's chuckle was so real in Ted's head that he glanced out the window to see if his brother was standing outside.

He was shocked when the words came out of his mouth and wondered if he'd actually said them. He cleared his throat and went on. "My name is Ted Wellman. My dad is Clayton Wellman, and he owns oil wells in this area. You might know him."

"Of course, I know Clayton. I host a poker game every few months and he joins us," the sheriff said.

"Where is this uncle who's saying Cassie"—Ted hoped he got that name right—"stole things from him?"

"Down near Sweetwater, Texas," the sheriff answered. "You sure this is your girlfriend?"

"Yes, sir, I am," Ted answered. "We've been dating for two years, but Cassie only has one uncle, and he lives up in Waurika, Oklahoma. He's about ninety and in a nursing home."

His lies just got bigger and bigger, but there was no backing out at this point.

The sheriff seemed to relax a bit, but then he smiled. Ted didn't know which was scarier—the hard-ass sheriff or the nice one. One could put him in jail for aiding and abetting a thief who had mental issues. The nice one could try to trip him up, and he'd end up in jail for the same reason.

"So, you're Clayton Wellman's son?" Bud cocked his head to one side and stared hard at Ted. "I can see that now. You look like him when he was younger. He's some poker player. I still owe him a hundred dollars that I haven't paid back."

"I'll tell him I saw you," Ted said. "Bud Tucker, right?"

Bud hitched his thumbs in his gun belt and swayed back and forth. "That's right, and because he plays a mean hand of poker and I know him, I'm going to do you kids a favor. My brother is the justice of the peace down in Montague. I'll just lead the way in my cruiser, and you two kids can get married in his office right across the street from the courthouse. And while you're getting hitched, I'll get you a room at a hotel in Nocona for the night. My sister runs a little motel over there. When you get home, you tell your dad that Bud Tucker paid that hundred dollars he owed him, and that I'm ready for another poker game when he gets back down here."

Cassie squeezed Ted's hand even harder, but he couldn't change the game now. If he did, the sheriff would win. Cassie would lose. He would get put so far away that not even his uncle Ash, the family lawyer, would be able to bail him out.

"Well, this *is* our lucky day." Ted grinned. "The sheriff owes my dad money, and we get a free honeymoon. Can't beat a deal like that. Lead the way, gentlemen." He pulled the woman up to stand beside him and draped his arm around her shoulders. She was even taller than she looked from a distance. Ted was six feet four inches tall, and he'd guess her to measure close to six feet—not totally unlike his sister, Liz.

"Didn't I tell you it would all work out, sweetheart?" He steered her outside to his battered pickup and opened the door for her.

She threw her backpack in between them on the bench seat and slid into the truck. "I'm not a thief, but I *am* a runaway. I'm twenty years old, and I have to find a place to hide until I'm twenty-one, which is only a few months from now, and I don't have an uncle." On the way from Lindsay to Montague, she gave him the short story of what had happened the last few years of her life. "I can't marry you. I don't even know you. What are we going to do to get out of this mess?" She began to wring her hands, and all the color left her face.

"Settle down, to start with." Ted thought she might faint any minute if she didn't calm down. "If the sheriff and his deputy don't go into the justice's office with us, we'll just tell the man we changed our minds and walk out. By the way, I really am Ted Wellman, and my dad is Clayton Wellman. And you are Cassie?"

"My name is Cassie Stewart," she answered. "What do we do if the sheriff does go into the justice's office with us?"

"We'll cross that bridge when we get to it," Ted answered. "Why didn't you just go get a job?"

"Because Cecil told me the trafficking ring he sold me to had already paid him half the money. He could get away with telling people I was a thief because I've lived with them since I was barely sixteen and never had a real job. I don't know why he said I had mental problems. I was valedictorian of my senior class in high school, and I studied to be a nurse's aide at the vo-tech school in Sweetwater. His place is ten miles out of town, and he sold Deana's car the day after she died. I had no transportation or money." Her voice cracked and she buried her face in her hands.

"Maybe we should just tell the sheriff what is really going on and let them bust open that sex ring," Ted suggested.

"You don't know Cecil. He's conniving, and believe me,

he would convince them that I stole from him and lied about him selling me. Thank God he doesn't know about my trust fund. Mama told me to never tell anyone, not even Deana, and I didn't." She clamped a hand over her mouth. "Please don't tell anyone."

"What trust fund?" Ted asked.

"My father and mother were never married, but he set up a fund for me to be given to me on my twenty-first birthday. Mama said that it was enough that I could go to nursing school if I still wanted to," Cassie said.

His uncle Ash's voice popped into Ted's head. *Is this woman telling you the truth, or is this a pack of lies? Is she a pathological liar?*

He gave Cassie a sideways glance, hoping to find answers in her expression, but all he saw were fear, confusion, and anger all balled up together and the tears streaming down her cheeks and dripping onto her denim jacket. A wave of sympathy washed over him, surprising him since he hadn't felt emotion—not love, hate, tears, joy, anger, or pain—in more than four years; not since John was killed when he lost control of his truck that fatal night.

Chapter 2

CASSIE STOLE LOOKS AT TED FROM THE CORNER OF HER EYE. His black hair reminded her of a raven's wing sparkling with highlights when the sunrays bounced off it. Gold flecks dotted his pecan-colored eyes, which were filled with worry. That was understandable. He didn't know her from any other stranger who'd walked into that store, and she could be just what Cecil had said about her—a thief, mentally challenged, and a liar.

When he'd draped an arm around her shoulders, she'd felt small and safe for the first time since she was fifteen. With those broad shoulders, he had probably played football in high school and maybe college, and if he ever crossed the California border, Hollywood would be waiting for him with open arms and a million-dollar contract.

"I'm not marrying you," she declared for a second time. "You could be a criminal. Or already married. I'll just let them put me in jail, call Cecil, and we'll sort out what we can when he shows up."

He shook his head. "I've never broken the law unless you count a couple of speeding tickets. I'm not married or engaged. I'm just a farmer from southern Oklahoma. But you *are* going to marry me, at least temporarily. I'd rather marry you—just for today—than go to jail for aiding and abetting a thief. My uncle can have it annulled tomorrow, and you can be on your way to wherever you were going. You will only be a bride for a day, so it's no big deal."

"Running away isn't a crime," she said through clenched teeth. "I'm not a thief. I only took what belonged to me out of Cecil's house. He's probably saying that the set of wedding rings that belonged to my grandmother was payment for letting me live in his house, but that's not true. They were in Deana's room, but they were always mine. My mother left them to me when she died." She wrapped her arms around the ratty denim purse in her lap. When she left the house ten miles out of Maryneal, she had wished that she had a suitcase, but now she was glad that she had packed what she could in the old backpack she had carried to high school. At least she had a couple of changes of clothing and her meager little makeup kit, and all her belongings hadn't gone with the bus.

"I believe you, and like I said, this is no big deal. I'm twenty-one years old, but my mama would take a switch to me if I didn't help someone in need," Ted said.

A black cat darted across the road in front of them, and Ted stomped on the brakes, throwing both of them forward. "I'm a little superstitious," he admitted.

"Me, too, and that means we're going to have bad luck." She groaned. "We won't be able to get out of this, will we? Nothing against you, and I'm glad that you're trying to help me, but I don't want to be a bride—not even for one day."

"Can't be helped." Ted sighed. "We're in too deep to crawl out now."

The black and white cruiser ahead of them stopped in front of a small white building across the street from the courthouse. A rusty pole supported a squeaky sign which needed a paint job as badly as the house did. The writing on the sign promised certified copies, said there was a notary public available, and offered weddings in fifteen minutes, all from Samuel T. Tucker, Justice of the Peace.

Bud and Tommy waved at them. "What happened back

there? Y'all weren't going to try to turn that truck around and outrun us, were you?"

"Oh, hell, no!" Ted shook his head.

"A black cat ran across the road in front of us," Cassie said.

"I'm sure glad it stayed on the side of the road until we got past," Tommy said. "I'm not superstitious about some things, but I'll drive a mile out of the way if a black cat crosses in front of me."

"That's a bunch of hogwash," Bud growled. "I forgot to ask you. You got your marriage license, didn't you?"

Cassie took a deep breath as she got out of the truck. "We thought we'd do that this morning and then get the judge to marry us."

Bud cracked up laughing. "Darlin', you have a three-day waiting period after you get your license at the courthouse. Didn't you know that? I guess maybe that black cat did bring you bad luck."

"No, we didn't know that." Ted groaned, but secretly, he heaved a sigh of relief. The charade was over, and the sheriff would have to let them go on their way. "Up in Oklahoma, we can get the license and get married all in the same day." Ted opened the truck door and got out. "Guess we'll have to go back across the Red River, sweetheart. I told you we should have gone to Vegas. They'll do all of it right there in the chapel."

"Why didn't you get married in Oklahoma?" Bud's expression changed from a smile to a frown.

"Her aunt works at the court clerk's office, and she don't like me." Ted, always the good twin and the shy one who never got into trouble, didn't realize a lie could fall out of his mouth so easily.

"We ain't got the money to be flittin' off to Vegas," Cassie said. "Looks like we'd better go to the courthouse and get a license and come back in three days."

Bud rubbed his chin. "I suppose I could get a waiver, but if I do, Clayton Wellman owes me a fifth of Gentleman Jack bourbon."

"Maybe that picture that Cecil Gorman is hunting up to put with his missing person's report has come in," the deputy said. "I think we should detain these two until we see if this is the woman who robbed him or not."

"I know Clayton, and a son of his wouldn't lie," Bud argued. "But"—he grinned—"why *are* you two eloping? I wouldn't want to go against a friend's wishes. Clayton and I are too good of buddies for me to do that. Is he against this marriage?"

"No, sir." Ted swallowed hard. His mind spun around in circles trying to find a way out of this new situation. "But Cassie's folks are. They don't think I'm good enough for her."

"Well, then hell's bells." Bud chuckled. "Let's go get that license and the waiver and come on back here for a weddin'. Just leave your truck parked right there, and we'll walk over to the courthouse."

"Fine with me." Ted took Cassie's hand in his, and they followed the sheriff and deputy across the street. "It's sure nice of you to help us out, Sheriff."

"No problem. Glad to do it, but I'm glad the Red River is between me and this young woman's relatives if they go gunnin' for folks who helped y'all out." Bud opened the door to the courthouse and continued to lead the way to the court clerk's office. "Let's go in and get things fixed up, and then make a trip back to my brother's place to make it all legal."

Bud opened another door that had Court Clerk in gold on the window. "You will be sure to tell your daddy that I helped you, and he owes me that bottle of bourbon, right?"

"Yes, sir. I sure will," Ted agreed.

Bud told the lady behind the desk what he needed.

"I need picture IDs," she said, "and the fee is seventy-five dollars."

Ted whipped out enough bills to cover that and then pulled his driver's license from his wallet and handed it to her. She typed in what she needed and then held out a hand toward Cassie.

It took a minute for Cassie to dig her wallet out of her purse. Ted thought that time stood still while she searched. What would the sheriff do when he saw her name on the driver's license? Hopefully, the lady wouldn't say Cassie Stewart right out loud, but would just type in her name like she had done with Ted's.

Finally, Cassie handed the woman her driver's license, and sure enough, the woman just typed in the name on the license. Ted was careful to let all the pent-up air in his lungs out very slowly so that the sheriff didn't question him about that too.

When the lady finished filling out the forms on the computer and printed them out, she handed them along with a receipt to Ted. "Good luck to you both. May you have a long and happy marriage," she said with half a smile.

"Now, let's go on back over and let Sam do the official business," Sheriff Bud said. "Then we'll take you kids to Nocona for your honeymoon night. It ain't the Ritz, but you'll have one night before you have to break the news to Cassie's relatives."

"Thank you." Ted nodded. "Is there a flower shop nearby so I could buy my beautiful bride a bouquet? A lady should have flowers on her wedding day, even if she doesn't have the big white dress and three-tiered cake."

Cassie's brain went numb for the second time in only an hour. What could Ted be thinking? He could turn around at any second and tell the law officers he didn't know who she was and walk away from it all. What would she do if after they had said the wedding vows, he expected her to be really married to him in every sense of the word?

"No problem," Bud said. "The best flower shop in town is across the street on the other side of the square. My cousin Rosie owns it. You kids go on over there, and we'll wait for you at Sam's place. Tell Rosie I sent you."

"Why did you do that?" Cassie whispered as they left the courthouse building and headed for a tiny shop with ROSIE'S FLOWERS AND GIFTS on the window.

"Removes all doubt from their minds," Ted said out of the side of his mouth.

Cassie attributed the light-headedness to hunger and the sparks flitting around her at Ted's touch to pure nerves. She felt as if she was somehow in a dream world. Any minute, she would wake up. She only hoped when she did that she was back in the trailer house with her mother and not in Cecil's place.

"What kind of flowers do you want?" Ted asked.

"I can't let you buy me a bouquet," Cassie protested.

"No letting me," Ted said. "It's all part of the program to keep us both out of jail. You for running away and being a thief. Me for aiding and abetting you. You like roses? If so, what color?" He opened the door and stood to the side to let her enter first.

"That one." She pointed at a silk flower arrangement of calla lilies and baby's-breath.

A gray-haired lady came from the back room with a pair of scissors in one hand and a knife in the other. "Hello. I'm Rosie. Can I help you?"

"Sheriff Bud Tucker said to tell you hello, and we'll take that bouquet right there." Ted dropped Cassie's hand and pointed.

"Honey, that is just a demo, and it's been in the shop for six months," she said. "Are you looking for something for a wedding?"

The phone rang, and a surge of fear rushed through Ted. Maybe that picture of Cassie had come through on the computer and Rosie was being told to hold them until the sheriff could get over there to arrest them. The woman was holding two weapons—one in each hand—and even though Oklahoma had an open carry law and Ted sometimes wore a gun on his hip, he never took it out of state with him.

"Yes, Amos," Rosie said. "I'd love to have a cheeseburger for supper. Can you remember to get tater tots with that instead of fries? Thanks, darlin'."

Ted hoped that wasn't code for *hold the people in your shop*, but was really a call from Amos, whoever he was.

"My husband, bless his heart, is running into Nocona on an errand," Rosie explained. "He's being a sweetheart and getting me a cheeseburger. He knows how much I love those things from the Dairy Queen there."

"Me too." Ted tried to keep his voice calm and collected. "Now, did you decide if we can buy that bouquet or not."

"I could just carry a single rose with some ribbons around it," Cassie suggested.

"Eloping, are you?" Rosie smiled.

"Yes, ma'am," Ted answered. "And Sam is waiting for us to get back over to his office."

"Got your rings yet?" Rosie glanced down at Cassie's hand.

"I guess that's another thing we forgot," Ted answered.

"I tell you what I'll do for you kids." She grinned. "You

buy your wedding bands from me, and I'll toss that bouquet in for free." She pulled a case of gold bands out from under the counter. "What size do you wear, darlin'?"

"Maybe a five," Cassie answered.

She remembered her granny saying, *You've got little fingers like me. Rest of me is tall and big-boned, but I've always just took a size five in rings.*

Could it have been just this morning that she walked into the pawn shop with those rings in her hand? It seemed like days, maybe even months ago.

"Small hands for such a tall girl," Rosie said.

"Pick out the ones you want," Ted told her.

"We shouldn't spend money like this, but those will do fine." She pointed to a pair of slim, very plain gold bands.

"Good taste," Rosie said as she removed the rings and put them in a velvet box. "That will be two hundred thirty dollars plus tax. Credit or cash?"

"Credit card." Ted slipped his card into the machine and signed the screen.

"Thank you and be happy," Rosie said. "Don't forget to pick up that bouquet. Would you like me to freshen it up with some new ribbons?"

"No, ma'am, this will do just fine. Don't want to keep

Sam waiting, and the sheriff and his deputy are going to be our witnesses." Ted stuffed the velvet box into his pocket and handed the bouquet to Cassie.

"Well, that's mighty sweet of Bud," Rosie said as she followed them to the door. "Tell him that Rosie says hello."

"Yes, ma'am," Ted said.

"This is all surreal," Cassie whispered as they walked back across the courthouse lawn. The sound of birds singing in the trees rang out. People came out of the courthouse, and others went in, sometimes stopping to visit, but most of the time rushing to their vehicles. Dark clouds overhead threatened rain or snow, and a cold north wind blew a few hairs across Cassie's face that had escaped her ponytail. "I feel like I'm going to wake up any minute and find myself back at Deana's place, or maybe I should say Cecil's."

"It'll be over in a few minutes, and tomorrow morning we can go home, get an annulment, and this will just be a story we tell our grandkids someday in the distant future." Ted tried to reassure her, but it fell short.

"I don't intend to ever get married for real," Cassie said, "so there will be no grandchildren for me. Since I'm an only child, and my mother was an orphan until Granny adopted her, there won't even be nieces or nephews."

"I can't imagine life without a family," Ted said.

When they reached the porch, Cassie balked. Ted gave her hand a gentle tug.

"We can do this and then we can undo it. Put on a smile and act like you're in love with me."

"I guess there's no other way, is there?" She grimaced.

"Only a jail cell," he whispered.

"Okay, then, let's do this." She squared up her shoulders, pasted on a smile, and went inside with Ted.

"Ready?" Bud asked.

"Yes, sir," Ted answered.

"Sam, you want to do this in your office or out here?" Bud yelled.

"In the office." Sam's high, squeaky voice came from across the hallway. "Rosie just called and said the kids were on the way."

"Yep." Bud motioned for them to go on into a room across the hallway. "They just arrived. Ted here has the marriage license in his hand, and his bride is the one with the bouquet."

"I think I could see the difference in the two," Sam said when they reached his small office.

Samuel Tucker was a short, fat man with bulldog jowls

that hung down on either side of his mushy lips. His slick, round head was as bald as a pumpkin, and it didn't look like it had ever sprouted a single hair. It was easy to see that he and Bud were brothers. They were built alike and had the same round face.

"Wedding license and waiver look all right. But I gotta see some other ID," Samuel said.

Ted dug in his pocket for his wallet again.

"Theodore Ashton Wellman, age 21," Samuel said aloud as he looked at the driver's license and then up at Ted. "How 'bout you, miss?" Samuel asked Cassie.

She pulled out her billfold and showed him her driver's license.

"Cassandra Elizabeth Rose O'Malley. Whew!" Sam chuckled. "That's a long name. Let's see now, your age is twenty, so you're of the legal age to get married in the state of Texas too. My fee is a hundred dollars to do a hurry-up wedding like this. Got to do a little more paperwork to file both the license and the waiver, you know."

Cassie said a silent prayer of thanks that neither she nor her mama had ever officially changed her name when her mama went back to using her maiden name of Stewart. Cassie had adopted it to make life simpler and Cecil had never been the wiser. Now that simple decision might be saving her life. She sighed.

━━━━━━━

Without a word, Ted took several bills from his wallet and laid them on top of the marriage license form. Sam laid the license to the side and stuffed the money into his shirt pocket.

Ted's chest ached, but he willed himself to act normal. His mouth felt like it was filled with cotton, but he had to keep his cool or he might end up sharing a jail cell with Cassie instead of a motel room.

Ladies had jitters, not full-grown twenty-one-year-old men. If his twin brother had been alive, John would have pulled a stunt like this without blinking an eye, and then bragged about fooling a county sheriff. He had always been the daredevil who thought he could cheat death, and the charmer who could sweet-talk the underpants off a holy woman. Ted had always been the one in the background, the shy one who had little to say.

Sam commenced the ceremony, speaking rapidly.

"Do you, Theodore Ashton Wellman, take Cassandra Elizabeth Rose O'Malley to be your lawful wedded wife, for better or for worse, in sickness or health..." Sam droned on and on.

Ted thought about his brother every day, sometimes every single hour. That day he wondered if circumstances had been different and he and Cassie had met in a quite different setting, would John have liked her? His twin brother had always gone for tall blondes, and Cassie was a redhead with a sprinkling of freckles across her nose, but still, would John have been standing beside him if Ted was getting married for real? They had said when they were just kids that neither of them would even think of settling down until they were thirty.

"Well, do you?" Sam asked loudly.

Ted jumped like he'd been shot. "I do," he almost shouted.

"Do you, Cassandra..." Sam went on with the ceremony.

Ted looked over at Cassie to find that the color had drained out of her face and her eyes were slightly glazed over. *Just don't faint or try to run!* He tried to get his message to her through osmosis, but she seemed to get paler by the second.

Please let us get through this and back out into the truck before she faints, Ted prayed.

She had said that she didn't want to ever get married, but Ted wondered if that was the truth. Had she envisioned herself in a church, standing beside a man who'd swept her off her feet, who had promised to give her the sun, the moon, and all the stars? Did she wish she was wearing a white satin gown, not a faded red sweatshirt, well-worn sneakers, and bleached-out jeans?

"Do you?" Sam asked.

"I do," she whispered.

"Rings?" Sam asked.

Ted pulled the box from his pocket, opened it, and removed the wedding bands.

"Well, well, well," the sheriff said. "I guess y'all really were down here to elope. I figured you'd come clean and say that this was all a hoax when the time came to really get married."

Ted slipped the ring on Cassie's finger, and she slipped the matching one on his. "With this ring, I thee wed," he said and she whispered.

"Guess that about does it except for the witnesses signing the license, and then I'll get it over to the courthouse and register it," Sam said. "Oh, you can kiss the bride now, son."

Ted looked down into Cassie's green eyes. He drew her close to him, tipped her chin back with his hand, and kissed her hard enough to convince that fool sheriff—and was surprised when Cassie kissed him back. He felt a surge of electricity course through him and thought that it was surely nothing more than relief that the charade was over.

"Okay. She can consider herself kissed," Sheriff Tucker said. "Tommy, let's lead the way over to the motel in Nocona and give them the keys to their honeymoon room. I called my sister while we were waiting for you, and she said she's putting you right next to the ice machine. That way if you want to run out and get some champagne"—Bud winked—"or maybe just beer, you won't have to go far to find ice for them."

Ted wondered if the sheriff had yet another relative who owned the local liquor store but decided not to ask.

_____

Cassie was speechless with anger, mostly at herself. She crossed her arms, huffed, and stomped the floor of the pickup as Ted drove behind the now all-too-familiar cruiser. Tears ran down her cheeks, and she felt like she'd just swallowed a stick of dynamite with a short fuse.

"That was a pretty convincing kiss for two people who've only known each other for an hour, don't you think?" he asked.

She slapped the dashboard and then bent forward and began to cry. "Dammit! I really am stupid."

"Hey." Ted patted her arm. "Was my kiss all that bad?"

"The kiss"—she sobbed even louder—"was"—she put her hands over her face and hiccupped—"just fine."

"Don't cry," Ted said in an attempt to soothe her. "Come on now. Hush. I told you that my uncle is a lawyer, and he'll undo this as soon as we get home. Please don't cry. I can't stand to see a lady cry. Besides, what will Bud and Tommy say if you're in tears when we get to our little love nest?"

"Hush!" Cassie pointed an accusing finger at him. "Don't you dare tease me. I'm sorry I ever saw you. Or got myself into this marriage." She sobbed even harder.

"I seem to remember that it took both of us," Ted replied.

"You are right, but none of it had to happen, Ted. Not one damn bit of it..." Cassie struggled for self-control so she could explain why she was crying so hard.

"Wipe those tears away and calm down, please, ma'am," he said and handed her his handkerchief.

"You've been so good to me, and I appreciate it, but none of this should have happened—and don't call me 'ma'am.' That makes me feel old, but I wish I was old. I wish I was past twenty-one and had whatever my inheritance is so I could be independent. I hate this feeling." She wiped her eyes with the hanky and gave it back to him.

He parked behind the sheriff's car in front of the motel, removed a pair of sunglasses from the sun visor, and handed them to her. "Put these on so they can't see your eyes. You don't want good ol' Bud and Tommy to start asking a million questions, now do you?"

Her thoughts were so scrambled that she could hardly latch on to one. Why was he so calm and nice? She had explained to him about her name, hadn't she? Or had she? She couldn't remember much right then past the time when all this fiasco had started during the bus stop.

Ted grabbed his suitcase and carried it around to the other side of the truck. He opened the door and held out a hand to help Cassie out of the truck. She picked up her backpack and purse and made a determined effort to smile at the waiting officers, but it came out more like a grimace.

Bud got out of the car, made a quick trip through the motel office, and then led the way down to Room 112. "Here it is. Lovers' paradise. You kids have a good night, and I'll expect that bottle of bourbon by the end of next week." He swung the door open with a flourish and tossed the key on the bed.

"I will, and thanks for everything." Ted dropped his

suitcase by the door and took Cassie's backpack and purse from her and did the same with them. Then he scooped Cassie up in his arms and carried her over the threshold.

"Was that necessary?" she asked, but she hung on to him even after they were in the room. "Are they really leaving? Are we rid of them at last?"

"I believe we are." Ted set her down in the middle of the floor.

He went back to the open door and picked up his suitcase and her backpack and kicked the door shut with the heel of his cowboy boot. He dropped his suitcase down on the floor, tossed her backpack on the bed, and locked the door.

"It's not too bad. I wouldn't give it a five-star review, but it'll do for the night," he said.

Cassie sat down on the edge of the king-size bed that took up a good portion of the room. There wasn't a wet bar, or even a tiny refrigerator and microwave like she'd seen in hotel rooms on the television, but there *was* a comfortable-looking recliner over in the corner and a big television on the wall. Cassie had never been in a hotel room before, so to her it looked pretty damned good, and the best thing was that the sheriff and his sidekick were gone.

"I can sleep in the recliner, and you can have the bed,"

Ted offered. "Or maybe we can just sneak out when Bud and Tommy are gone for sure."

"Oh, Ted," she groaned as she threw herself backwards and curled up in a ball.

"Now what did I do?" he asked in exasperation. "I said we could get this marriage undone tomorrow. I kept those two characters from sending you back to wherever it is you're running from. Why are you mad at me?"

She sat up and wiped away still more tears with the bottom of her shirt. "Ted, I am an O'Malley," she said.

He just stared at her with a blank look on his face. Was he the one who had mental issues? Didn't he understand the significance of what she was saying?

"You *were* an O'Malley. So? Now you're legally a Wellman, and tomorrow you can be an O'Malley again. So what?" He opened his suitcase.

"Those lawmen are looking for Cassie Stewart," she explained. "My mother's maiden name was Stewart, and even though I'm legally an O'Malley since that was my dad's name, I went by Stewart. Cecil doesn't even know my legal name. Don't you see? If I had been able to think straight, I could've just shown them my driver's license which says I'm an O'Malley in that con-venience store. But I was so scared I wasn't thinking right."

"Sweet Jesus!" Ted gasped.

"The sheriff was looking over my shoulder when I pulled out the license in the courthouse, and since the lady didn't say my name out loud, I still wasn't thinking straight. Then the JP asked for an ID, and it dawned on me, but things had gone too far by then. I was afraid that they would put us in jail for lying to a police officer."

"What's done is done," Ted told her.

"If I had half a brain, I wouldn't be married to you and I'd be on that bus to Oklahoma City. I'm so sorry to have messed up your life like this. And you could already be back in whatever town you said you were from." Cassie sighed.

"It's not one of those things that can't be undone," Ted said.

"But it was all so unnecessary," she moaned.

"Why don't you take a nice, warm shower. Do you have a nightshirt or something to wear in that backpack? I've got a clean T-shirt right here if you need it." He pulled a shirt from his luggage and held it up. "I really was in Waco last night picking up oil-well parts. I knew I'd have to spend the night, so I brought extra things with me."

"I don't need it." She'd taken enough from him, and besides, that T-shirt wouldn't reach down past her underpants.

If he thought for one minute she was going to be a real wife to him that night, he had another think coming. She wasn't sure about the law, but if they consummated the marriage, it might complicate an annulment. And besides, Cassie did not sleep with guys she just met that day.

"You need to unwind and relax. Go take a shower or a long bath. My sister says that helps her when she's all stressed out," Ted said.

"I'm not so sure a bath is going to just wash away all my stress." Sarcasm dripped from every word out of her mouth. She changed her mind and headed toward the bathroom. The room did a couple of spins, and then she was reaching out to grab something to keep her from falling. All she got was an armful of air, and then strong arms wrapped around her and went down with her.

"Cassie, wake up. Open your eyes, girl. If you don't wake up, I'm calling 911."

She could hear his voice, but it sounded like it was out there in the mesquite grove behind Deana's house. Was Deana all right? He said he was calling 911, so that had to mean she was in trouble. Her eyes fluttered open and she caught a glimpse of his worried face. Who was this man, and why was he holding her? Then her eyes closed again.

"Come on, Cassie," he whispered. "Wake up or else I'm taking you to the emergency room."

"No! I don't have money for doctors…" she mumbled. "I'm just hungry. No food for days."

Ted stood up with her still in his arms and laid her down on the bed. "How long has it been since you've eaten?"

"Can't remember," she said without opening her eyes. "Is this Thursday? Didn't get to eat yesterday because Cecil was mad. Tuesday, maybe Monday. I had some milk Tuesday, I think."

"Listen to me." He bent over her and said, "Open your eyes for just a minute and listen to me."

She forced her eyes open and stared at him. It was Ted, and she had married him. No, that couldn't be right. She didn't know him. This was just a hallucination.

"I'm going to go buy food and bring it back. There's a Dairy Queen just down the road a little way. Burgers, chicken strips, tacos. Name your poison, but don't try to stand up. Promise me that you'll lie right here until I get back. You might get dizzy and faint again." Ted still sounded like he was talking from the bottom of a pit.

She nodded, but her eyes didn't open. "I promise, and I don't care what you get as long as it's food."

Ted sure hoped the sheriff wasn't around when he drove twenty miles over the speed limit to the Dairy Queen. He had often eaten there when he was out traveling for the farm or the oil company, so he knew the food and most of the help that worked there.

"It takes a lowlife to refuse to let a woman have food," he muttered as he skidded to a stop, leaving tire tracks in his wake as he slowed down to turn into the parking lot. "Dammit!" He slapped the steering wheel when he saw the sheriff's car parked right in front of the café, and there he was waving out the window at Ted.

"Talk about bad luck," Ted said as he waved back and then got out of the truck.

"You kids worked up an appetite already?" Bud yelled from one of the two booths in the back when Ted walked in. "Must be great to be young."

"Yes, sir, it really is." Ted forced himself to grin as he went to the counter and ordered two burgers, a chicken strip dinner, two chocolate shakes, and a couple of soft drinks.

"I'm looking forward to another poker game with your dad. You should come with him next time he's down this way," Sam hollered as Ted left with a sack full of food and a cardboard cup holder with his shakes and root beers.

"Sure will. Thanks for all you did for me and my—uh—wife." Ted almost tripped over the word.

"It'll take a while to get used to saying that word, son," Bud said, "but once you've had the old ball and chain wrapped around your leg for twenty years, it's easier to remember."

"And once your wife hits you a few times with the rollin' pin or a skillet, you really will remember the word wife," Tommy said, laughing.

"Hey, we got that picture of the runaway girl in, and she looks a lot younger than twenty and a little like Cassie, but not enough. Picture is pretty dark, though. Still, I couldn't arrest her on the basis of that photo," Bud said. "Better get going before those burgers get cold. You don't want the little woman mad at you on your wedding night."

"Yes, sir." Ted was glad to get outside and into his truck, but he made sure he didn't drive a single mile over the limit all the way back to the motel.

When he opened the door, Cassie was lying on the bed just like he had left her. He stared at her for several seconds and thought she might have died while he was out. She was so pale that she could be dead, but then she whimpered in her sleep and took a deep breath.

"Thank God," he muttered.

Explaining to his family how he had come by a wife was going to be a nightmare, but trying to tell them that she had passed away on their wedding night would be even worse.

"I don't want to wake up," she muttered. "I smell food, and I know it's just a figment of my imagination."

"No, it's not," Ted said. "Supper is here. Wake up and eat." He handed her a chocolate shake. "Take a few sips of this, and choose whatever you want from this, just don't eat too fast."

She ignored his advice and wolfed down a chicken strip and then picked up a burger. "I'd be embarrassed to eat like this if I wasn't half-starved," she said between bites. "Thank you so much. I thought for a few minutes I would faint right there during the marriage ceremony. I was so hungry that the room had begun to spin in circles."

"I can't imagine the life you lived with that man," Ted said.

"It wasn't so bad when Deana was alive"—Cassie sipped at the milkshake—"because he was gone a lot, but after she passed away, he was pure evil. I don't think anything has ever tasted as good as this food."

"I need to call my uncle Ash and kind of prepare him for what he's going to need to do for us. You just keep eating, and I'll step outside to make the call," Ted said. "Save me a burger."

"Lock the door and take the key with you. I'll have a shower when I get finished. If you don't mind, I *will* borrow that T-shirt you offered. I didn't bring anything to sleep in." She smiled at him for the first time since he'd put that gold ring on her finger.

Ted carried his cell phone outside, sat down on a park bench to the right of the door, and took several deep breaths before he finally got up the nerve to call his uncle.

"Uncle Ash, this is Ted," he said.

"You're late for supper, and your mama won't let us eat until you get here," Ash said. "Did you have trouble with that old truck? I've told you not to depend on that rattletrap, especially when you go out of state. You should have driven your new one."

"The truck is fine," Ted said. "I left Waco in plenty of time, b-but..." He stammered. "Something came up." He paused and scratched his head, trying to figure out just how in hell he was going to explain in a few words what he had done. "I'm in a jam. Maybe you and I can talk about it over breakfast tomorrow morning. I'm staying here tonight, but I'll be home early."

"I'll save you a couple of strips of bacon, then," Ash joked. "So, what kind of a jam are you in?"

Ted took another deep breath and blurted out, "I got married. And I need you to unmarry me as quick as you can."

"You did *what*?" Ash's tone went from his usual deep Texas drawl to sounding like a ten-year-old girl's voice.

"Shhh…" Ted said. "I don't want Mama and Daddy to know until I get home. It's a long story, and—"

"I'll keep it a secret until you get here, but…" Ash hesitated.

Ted heard footsteps and a door close.

"I've stepped outside so the others can't hear, but why would you get married and want to end it the next day? This sounds like something John would have done, but not you," Ash said in a low voice.

"I know," Ted said. "I was trying to help out this woman and it snowballed, but neither of us want to be married, so can you undo it?"

"I hope so. You're too young to be married. Where is this woman, and who is she?" Ash asked.

"In a motel room. I'm outside"—Ted sighed—"just like you are."

"If you really want an annulment, then don't sleep with her tonight," Ash cautioned.

"Don't plan on it," Ted told him. "And trust me, she wants out of this situation even more than I do. I'll bring her home tomorrow morning, and you can meet her then. We should be there in time for breakfast. You will be there, right?"

"I wouldn't miss those fireworks for all the tea in China and half the dirt in Texas!" Ash answered.

Chapter 3

CASSIE SET WHAT WAS LEFT OF HER MILKSHAKE ON THE nightstand before she went into the bathroom. She had planned on a quick shower, but she hadn't had a real soaking bath in years. There was only a shower in Deana's small bathroom, and it might be a long time before she could have a long bath again, so she adjusted the water, stripped out of her clothing, and sank down into the tub even before it was half-full.

If only I can hide out until Cecil gets tired of looking for me, she thought as the warm water covered her thin body. *If only I had insisted on going to college and not let him put that guilt trip on me. If only I had gotten a real job and saved my money rather than working for Deana for nothing.*

If only is a waste of your time. Her mother's voice popped into her head. *I gave you a miracle. Make the most of it.*

So Ted Wellman and being married was a miracle, was it?

"You all right in there?" Ted's voice followed a light knock on the door.

"I'm fine, and enjoying this bath," she called out.

"Okay, then, I'm going to turn on the television and get comfortable in the recliner," he said.

She stayed in the tub until the water went cold and then thought about running another bath, but in case Ted wanted a shower she didn't want to use all the hot water. She wrapped one of the four towels on the rack around her wet hair and one around her body. When she was dressed in clean underpants and Ted's T-shirt that smelled like the fabric softener she and Deana used at home, she peeked out the door into the room.

He had fallen asleep in the recliner, and the second burger was gone. She crossed the room, picked up a tater tot and popped it in her mouth, crawled under the covers on the bed, and let out a long sigh. This bed covered almost as much space as her whole bedroom in Deana's house. She felt like she had just cuddled down into an acre of big white fluffy clouds and it was all hers for that night.

"Feel better?" Ted asked without opening his eyes.

"Yes, I do, and thank you," she answered. "This bed feels like heaven, but that warm bath was even better."

"Good," he said. "This recliner isn't bad at all. I called home and told Uncle Ash what we wanted and needed. He'll keep it to himself until we get there, but there shouldn't be a problem. Want to watch television to pass the time?" Ted asked.

"Love to," Cassie said. "You can sit on the bed with me, Ted."

"Thanks, but I'm comfortable right here," he said. "I've already kicked off my boots and propped my feet up. The bed is all yours."

"Thanks…again"—she propped two pillows against the headboard and leaned back on them—"for everything, and I mean that, Ted. This is the first time since Deana died that I haven't been tied up in a ball of knots and nerves, and I feel safe."

"That's a good thing. I want you to feel like that, and guess what?" He went on to tell her that he'd run into the sheriff again, and that the picture Cecil had sent out was actually too dark for them to identify her with. "That means Cecil might go a different way even if he does come looking for you."

"That had to be the one of me taken when I was fifteen, right after my mama passed away. It was sitting on Deana's dresser, and you're right, it is dark. I was sitting in the shadow of the porch with one of her baby goats beside me," Cassie said.

"Well, we can thank goodness that he didn't have a more recent one. That just might be the break you need," Ted said and yawned.

Ted didn't even realize he'd fallen asleep until Cassie shook him awake at dawn. "Let's get going before the sheriff wakes up," she whispered. "I'm still afraid Cecil might figure out I came this way and follow me up here even though the picture doesn't look like me anymore. He'll check the bus schedules and even spin that story about me being a thief and having mental issues. He's very charming when he wants to be."

Ted cracked open one eyelid and saw that Cassie had turned on a bedside lamp. According to the alarm clock on the nightstand it was five thirty. His mama usually had breakfast on the table about six thirty, and they were only half an hour from the farm.

"Ouch." He rubbed his arm. "Guess I slept wrong. My

arm is tingling. I'll take a shower and brush my teeth, and then we'll scoot on out of here and across the Red River."

"How far is it to where you live?" Cassie asked.

"Maybe thirty minutes, but it's only about eighteen miles until we're in Oklahoma," he answered.

"Oh. My. Gosh!" she exclaimed. "I thought it was miles and miles. Why didn't we just go up there and get things started yesterday?"

"Because that would have sent up a red flag. We needed to stay here and check out this morning to keep things safe," he said on his way to the bathroom.

Ted turned the key in to the night clerk at the motel, loaded their things into his truck, and headed west on Highway 82. Cassie stared out the side window and didn't have anything to say, and Ted couldn't think of a single way to start a conversation. The old shy Ted had returned, leaving behind the adventurous cowboy who was willing to rescue a damsel in distress.

Ted was glad when he crossed the Red River into Oklahoma, leaving Sheriff Bud Tucker's jurisdiction behind, but the closer he got to home, the more he withdrew into his normal shell where he was comfortable. He had no doubt he had disappointed his parents with his decision to help Cassie, and he just couldn't bear to feel that pain.

"I appreciate your help, honest I do," Cassie said, "but we're out of Texas now, so why don't you just pull over and let me out? I can hitch a ride to Oklahoma City from here."

Ted slapped the steering wheel with both his hands and surprised himself at the outburst since he'd just decided to wallow around in his usual emotionless state. "Didn't your mama ever tell you what happens to girls who hitch rides? Don't you know better than to get in a car with a stranger?" His voice got louder with every word.

"Don't you dare shout at me!" she yelled right back. "*You're* almost a complete stranger. Mama told me lots of things, but I guess she didn't think to tell me not to marry a complete stranger. We both thought I had better sense than that!"

"Sorry I yelled," Ted said, "but I'm pretty sure we both have to be there to get an annulment. You'll have to sign papers, and this is Saturday so it's going to be Monday before the courthouse opens and we can get anything done. I'm sure you can stay with my family over the weekend. There is plenty of room."

"Okay, okay!" Cassie turned around to glare at him.

"You're nervous," Ted said. "I know because I'm just as nervous as you are. Talk to me. It will help pass the time.

You've told me about your mother and Deana and Cecil. Tell me about your father."

"My daddy was Patrick O'Malley. Granny Stewart told me I got my red hair and my temper from my father, but my green eyes were just like my mother's. My daddy had cancer, and Mama told me there was a problem with the insurance if they got married. She knew he was dying when they got together, but they fell in love and she got pregnant, and"— Cassie shrugged—"he left the life insurance money in a trust fund for me. I don't even know how much it is."

"And your grandmother?" Ted asked when she stopped talking.

"She passed away when I was about six years old. Mama said she hung on long enough to help take care of me until I was old enough to go to school," Cassie answered.

"I'm sorry." Ted had never seen anything more beautiful than the WELCOME TO RYAN, OKLAHOMA sign on the south end of town. Not even the fields covered in bluebonnets that he'd seen in Texas were as pretty as that sign. "Sounds like your grandmother meant a lot to you," he said as he made a right turn down Washington Street. Five more minutes and he would be home, and he dreaded every second of that time.

Cassie nodded. "My granny was everything to me. She

started teaching me my letters when I was three years old. It wasn't long before I was reading. She said I took to it like a duck to water. When she enrolled me in kindergarten, I was so far ahead of the other kids that they put me in the first grade. Granny was so proud. She said I'd be in college before she knew it." Cassie stopped and wiped away a tear.

"Hey," Ted said softly. "You don't have to tell me everything—especially if it upsets you. We can just ride along quietly," he said. "After the annulment on Monday, I'll take you wherever you want to go."

"Granny used to tell me that to understand today, you have to know about yesterday," she said in a dull voice. "Now you pretty much know everything about me, and all I know about you is that you have an uncle who is a lawyer and you are a dirt farmer."

Ted's stomach felt empty, but he wasn't hungry. He hadn't exactly been honest with Cassie. The Wellmans were a lot more than dirt farmers. They were one of the most influential families in Jefferson County. But that wasn't the problem with the way he felt. After all the lies he told Sheriff Bud, what he didn't tell Cassie could be considered covering up the truth.

He remembered feeling empathy before his brother died

and was surprised to feel it again. He'd thought he would never feel anything at all after that horrible night.

"So why are you going to Oklahoma City?" he asked. "Got friends there?"

"No friends in Oklahoma City. No family anywhere," she answered.

Everything was quiet again for several minutes, but Ted needed something to fill the heavy space in the truck, so he asked, "What did you do other than take care of Deana?"

"We made a garden, canned food, made jellies and jams from the strawberries and plums we harvested from the yard. West Texas is a hard land, and we had to fight it to get anything at all, but we managed to put away food for the winter months. She was too weak for the garden work this year, so I put her in a lawn chair, and I did the work. It will probably all die now. Cecil will leave on his truck runs and..." She shrugged. "I wanted to scatter her ashes over the garden because that was where she was happiest, but Cecil wouldn't hear of it. He said that he wanted to keep them on the buffet in the dining room to remember her. I can't imagine why since he tried to crawl into my bed that very night."

The closer they got to the farm, the more Ted's nerves felt like they were tied up in a knot. He had been numb for so many years that he had forgotten how it felt to have to face the music, as his dad often said, and yet his insides seemed to be reeling with a roller coaster of emotions.

"Are you really a farmer?" she finally asked, breaking another long silence.

"I am," he answered. "I have a few acres of my own right next to my dad's land." His dad who was going to skin him alive for marrying this girl. His uncles might even tack his hide to the smokehouse door to remind all future generations of Wellman males never to do anything so crazy again.

Maybe so, he thought, *but if they'd seen Cassie looking so lost and frightened, they would have done the same thing I did.*

"It's only two more miles. Daddy has always been an early riser, and my younger sister, Alicia, takes forever to get ready for school, so she has to get up before the crack of dawn, so she's used to being up early too."

"They're all going to hate me. You should have let me hitch a ride after we crossed the Red River."

"I don't have that kind of family, and you should know by now that I'm not going to hurt you, girl," Ted said. "Welcome home, Mrs. Wellman," Ted said as he pulled into a tree-lined lane that led up to a house that looked more like a hotel than a home.

"Home?" She tried to blink but her eyelids would not close.

She had expected a small frame house, the kind a dirt farmer in West Texas might have. One with peeling paint and a dirt yard with a beat-up car jacked up on concrete blocks and an old tractor peeking out from behind the house.

Instead, the place looked like a picture from one of those historical western romance novels Cassie liked to read sometimes. The farmhouse—if it could be called a mere farmhouse—was two stories high, with balconies and a wrap-around verandah. The landscaped yard was straight out of one of those gardening books her granny had spent hours looking at every spring. Lush green grass covered the yard. Roses bloomed in front of the house, and bright yellow and purple pansies mingled together in the flower beds.

"There's Uncle Ash's pickup." Ted pointed to a brand-new black club-cab truck parked in the driveway. "And Uncle Brock is here because that's his red Cadillac over there."

"Ash is the lawyer. Who is Brock?" Cassie whispered. "What do they all do for a living? Own a series of gold mines?"

"Uncle Ash is the lawyer who's going to unmarry us. Uncle Brock is a medical doctor and the town of Ryan's general practitioner. His wife, my aunt Maggie, works with him in the family clinic as his nurse. Ash and Brock are my daddy's brothers. My daddy owns some oil wells, and he runs an oil-well maintenance business too. But he started out as a farmer, the way I'm starting out."

"Why are they all here? I think you missed somebody. Who owns that white pickup truck?" she asked nervously.

"That's mine," Ted said. "This is the work truck that I use for trips to pick up oil-well parts. I don't want to scratch up my new truck. Would you have preferred to be rescued in the new one, kind of like a knight riding in on a white horse?"

"Not necessarily, but, Ted, I'm really nervous now. I didn't even think about you being rich," she said.

"I'm just a cowboy who's been blessed with some lucky breaks," he said. "Let's go on inside and introduce you to my family."

Ted got out of the truck, helped Cassie out of the passenger side, and then held her hand as they climbed the stairs onto the front porch. She stopped like she had at the JP's office the day before, but Ted didn't drag her inside.

"Okay, I'm ready," she said after a few seconds, "but don't expect miracles."

"We don't need them in this house." Ted opened the huge double doors.

She didn't attempt to pull her hand away, not because she wanted his folks to think she was really married to him, but to steady her nerves.

His father, Clayton Wellman, waved from the sofa in the living area of the great room. He must have realized Ted was standing inside the door with a woman and dropped the paper on the floor. Brock was sitting on the sofa with his wife, Maggie, right beside him. Ash laid his cell phone to the side and stared at Ted like he had grown horns or maybe an extra eyeball in the middle of his forehead since he left Oklahoma two days ago.

A young girl with thick, dark hair piled on top of her head in a messy bun came from the kitchen. Her brown eyes registered shock, and she locked eyes with Cassie. "Ted? What's going on?"

Good grief! Was this someone Ted was dating? The woman looked like she could drop Cassie with nothing more than a glare.

"Hello, Nephew," Ash said in a loud, booming voice. "Bring your new wife in and introduce us to her."

"You got married? I don't believe it!" The young woman's voice went all high and squeaky. "If this wasn't you, I'd think it was a joke you are pulling. If it is, it's not funny. How much did he pay you to do this? Whatever it was, it's not enough." She whipped around to air-slap her brother on the arm. "You are not married. Take her back to wherever you rented her from."

"I'm not that kind of person, and he did not rent me." Cassie let go of Ted's hand and bowed up to the short woman. "Yes, he married me, but only because it was that or go to jail. Now, let's get this annulment over with, and I will leave."

"Wife!" His mother whispered from the kitchen doorway, and then smiled as if it was good news. Long dark hair, streaked just slightly with gray, was pulled back in a low ponytail at the nape of her neck. She wore a denim skirt and a red sweater, both covered with a bibbed apron with lace on the edges.

"Yes, wife—at least for a day." Ted's voice and the expression on his face told Cassie that he damn sure didn't want to have to tell his folks what had happened.

Cassie took a step forward. "It's like this."

"No, wait," Ted said. "Let me introduce you before we tell them the story. Everyone, this is Cassie, and Cassie, this is my uncle Ash. The one who was reading the paper is my dad. The couple on the sofa are my uncle Brock and aunt Maggie and this"—he nodded toward his sister—"is my sister, Alicia. And that's my mother, Maria."

"I'm pleased to meet you, Cassie." Maria crossed the room and hugged Cassie. "Ash said you were bringing home a surprise, Son, but we weren't expecting something this big. Come on in the living room and tell us the story. We didn't even know you were dating someone."

"Hello, everybody." Cassie straightened her back and stood tall. "I'm real sorry to barge into your home without explanation, but before Ted explains, I want all of you to know I appreciate what Ted has done to help me out. Now if you'll just show me where to sign the papers, I'll be on my way."

"What papers?" Maria asked.

"Let me explain," Ted said.

"I think you better do just that, Son," his father said.

Ted started at the beginning, from when he'd looked up and seen Cassie for the first time barely twenty-four hours ago, and he didn't stop until he'd told it all, including that she'd fainted from hunger, but he left out the parts about Cecil and her past. That was her story to tell, not his.

When he finally finished, Cassie needed one of those fans that her granny used to fan her face in the summertime. It had a picture of Jesus on one side and an advertisement for the funeral home on the back. She couldn't help but wonder which one she was destined for in the next five minutes.

She could feel Maria's eyes on her—even more than those of Jesus on the cardboard fan with a Popsicle stick for a handle. When Ted had finished with his story, Maria smiled, which surprised Cassie. She should be screaming at her son, not smiling at him.

"I'm so proud of you, Son," Maria said. "Ash can take care of the annulment, I'm sure, but it will take time. Cassie will stay with us until it's all finished, and, Brock, you said last week that you need an aide in the clinic. This girl needs a job. She can start work for you on Monday morning."

Cassie wasn't sure she'd heard any of that right. Ted's mother should be throwing a hissy fit, not inviting a strange woman into her home or finding her a job. And not one of those grown men was telling Ted that he was crazy to get involved with a total stranger. What exactly was wrong with this picture?

Clayton was the first one to chuckle; then that turned into infectious laughter and pretty soon all three men were guffawing. Finally, Clayton stopped long enough to wipe his eyes. "Has your brother's spirit come back and jumped into your body? This is something John would do, not you."

"It's not funny." Ted slumped down on the sofa.

Cassie wasn't sure if she should continue standing or

sit, but finally Alicia took her arm and led her to a chair. "Evidently, my brother is all out of whatever it takes to rescue a damsel in distress. Here, have a seat."

Cassie eased down into the chair. Were these people totally out of their minds? First, Ted's mother hugged her, and then the guys in the room thought it was funny that he married her. This was no laughing matter—not to Cassie.

"I'm not looking for handouts," she said loud enough that they all stopped talking and stared at her. "I didn't want to be married. I didn't even want to come here, but Ted said it would require both of us to get the annulment. So give me something to sign and I'll be gone."

Cassie caught the look that passed across the face of Ash, a tall guy with the same color eyes as Ted's. He and both of his brothers, Clayton and Brock, had high cheekbones and a face that a painter or a sculptor would love.

The smile left Ash's face and he became serious. "It's not a handout if you work for it."

"And I really do need help at the clinic," Brock said.

"You'd hire me without even checking to see if I really finished the courses to be a nurse's aide?" Cassie asked.

"Oh, honey, we will definitely call the school and get them to fax your transcript and list of classes to us," Maggie told her. "That's just standard practice, but Brock is right. Ryan is a small place and getting a qualified aide with experience like you've had isn't easy to find. Plus, you drove through the town. Not many people would want to live here."

"We'll check your credentials on Monday," Brock said. "If everything is good, you can start on Tuesday morning."

"You can stay here with us until the annulment comes through," Maria told her.

"Thank you." Cassie wanted to call Deana and tell her that she was going to work in a clinic, that at last she was going to get to use the education she'd gotten at the vo-tech school to do what she had always wanted.

Deana is gone, the voice in her head reminded her.

"You can help me with breakfast every morning to pay for your room and board. This whole crew is in and out all the time, and I can use some help, so it's not as if you'd be accepting charity," Maria said. "But for now, breakfast is on the bar, so let's all gather round and have a good hot meal. After that I'll show Cassie up to Lizzy's old room. I think she'll be comfortable there. You can save some money, and after Ash figures out how to end this marriage, you can go anywhere you like."

"Do you have scrubs?" Maggie asked.

Cassie shook her head. "If I could work in jeans, I'll buy some with my first paycheck."

Everything had happened fast—too fast. Living with Cecil, even for a few days a month, had taught her to read people, but when she glanced over at Ted, his face was totally blank.

"Thank you all for these kind offers, but I can't do this. Ted has been too good to me, getting me out of trouble and then standing beside me. It's not right for him to put his life on hold. If I'm gone, no one other than the people in this room will even know about this fake marriage. He can go on with his life. Surely, there's a form I can sign that can be used for the annulment, isn't there?" she asked.

"We've already had this conversation." Ted didn't yell, but his tone was serious. "I wouldn't feel right about you hitchhiking anywhere, especially when you have no one to stay with when you get to wherever you were going."

"Are you a churchgoing person?" Maria asked.

"Before Mama died, we drove up to Sweetwater on Sundays. First we'd go to early morning mass, and then to Walmart for whatever we needed that week, and then on the way home we'd get a burger for lunch. Mama had to be back by eleven to start her shift at the diner." Cassie's eyes misted at the memory, but she stiffened her back and refused to let these people see her cry.

Maria's smile got bigger, and Alicia sat down on the arm of the chair. "You might as well do what Mama wants. She always gets her way, and I hate to admit it, but she's almost always right."

"Do you remember that verse from catechism classes that talks about not being forgetful to entertain strangers, because you might entertain angels unawares?" Maria asked.

It took a moment for Cassie to realize what Maria was saying. "I'm not an angel. I'm not a thief, and I'm not mentally challenged like Cecil says I am. I only took what belonged to me when I left."

"We don't need to hear your whole life story," Maria said, "but we would feel horrible if harm came to you because we weren't hospitable."

Brock pulled his wallet from his back pocket and took out two hundred dollars. "Here's an advance on your salary. Ted can drive you up to Duncan later today, and you can get some pink scrubs if you want to work for me. There are only three of us in the office right now. I'm the doctor. Maggie is the nurse, and Gloria manages our office. We really need another person to help us out."

Ted took the money from Brock's hand and offered it to Cassie. "We'd all feel better if you did what Mama wants you to do."

Cassie nodded and accepted the bills from him. This wasn't a handout or charity, she told herself. It was a job and a hiding place. Her mother *had* really sent down a miracle for her.

Chapter 4

"THIS IS MY BIG SISTER LIZ'S OLD ROOM." ALICIA OPENED the door to a bedroom almost the size of the small house Cassie had lived in with Deana. "She got married a few years ago, but Momma kept everything pretty much as it was. My room's right across the hall if you ever need anything. Or just want to talk sometime." She headed back out into the hallway.

"Thank you, but please wait," Cassie said. "Why are you treating me so nice? You should be yelling at me for ruining your brother's life. He'll always be tagged as the guy who married a woman and then got it annulled the next week. He could be the laughingstock of your whole town. Isn't that a bad thing? It would have been out in West Texas where I lived. Maryneal, where I was born and grew up, only has about two hundred people in the whole community, and believe me, this kind of story would be talked about for years."

"When my brother John—that would be Ted's twin—died, Ted retreated into a shell. That was when he was sixteen, and we haven't seen emotion out of him since that night. He just retreated into himself and never grieved like the rest of us did. The first step in that process is denial. Ted is still stuck right there and hasn't moved on. We'll always miss John, but we've accepted that he is gone. Not Ted. I believe he figures if he just thinks John is gone for the day that he doesn't have to face that he is gone forever," Alicia said. "He seldom smiles, and even I can't make him mad enough to yell at me."

"What has that got to do with me?" Cassie asked. "And he can yell. I promise. I heard him."

"He rescued you, and when he told us about you being so hungry that you fainted, we saw tears in his eyes," Alicia told her. "Part of him died when John did. He is still the shy twin, the one who helps the neighbors get their hay in if it was going to rain, who works from daylight to midnight on the land, but it's like he's numb and can feel nothing."

"He argued with me, more than once," Cassie said.

"That's why we want you to stay with us for a while. This is a miracle to us, and we're grateful to you," Alicia said.

"How did John die?" Cassie asked.

"In a wreck. He was racing with another guy and lost control of his truck. I felt like I lost both of my brothers that day, but a little bit of one came back to me this morning," Alicia answered with a sigh. "I'm going now to let you get settled in, but..." Alicia crossed the room and hugged Cassie. "Thank you, and I'm sorry I said those things about you when you first got here," she whispered and then turned and left the room before Cassie could say a word.

Cassie turned around slowly several times, trying to take in everything about the room. Deana said that where a person stayed defined them. That was when she was trying to talk Cassie into making the tiny bedroom personal with pictures or posters on the wall or knickknacks on the dresser. Deana had even offered to let her have her choice of the bright-colored quilts she had made to go on her twin-size bed, but Cassie had refused.

Even after the pale-blue chenille bedspread was thread-bare, she continued to use it because she imagined that it smelled like her mother's hand lotion. Every night before Cassie went to sleep, Frannie, her mother, had come into her bedroom and kissed her on the forehead. When she was a little girl, the kiss kept the monsters away, and the scent of her mother's hand lotion, a mixture of cherry and almond, stayed behind. Cassie always thought that it was that scent that kept the monsters at bay, not the kiss.

A white rocking chair sat in the corner, and a white eyelet comforter covered the four-poster bed. Evidently Liz liked pastels, because the sheer drapes were pink and the throw pillows were pale blue, minty green, lavender, and shades of pink. French doors led out onto one of the balconies, and after wondering if she should even sit in a pristine white rocking chair or lie on the bed, Cassie needed a breath of fresh air.

She pulled back the sheer drapes, opened the balcony door, stepped outside, and sat down in one of the two chairs that were placed in the corners of the small landing. The view was gorgeous out across acres of land and a small pond with ducks floating on the top of the water. Half a dozen little yellow-colored babies paraded behind their mama. Cassie couldn't hear them, but she imagined they were tattling on one another as their little beaks opened and shut.

"Mama, Alicia just said I am the miracle. I thought Ted was. Can we both be?" she said barely above a whisper.

She didn't hear the door open or anyone walking across the carpet, so when Maria spoke, Cassie almost jumped out of her skin.

"I didn't mean to startle you." Maria came out onto the balcony and sat down. "I knocked but you didn't answer, so I peeked in and saw that you were out here. I wanted to tell you that Liz is about your size, and she left some things behind in her closet when she got married and moved out. I've been meaning to donate them to the church clothes closet but just haven't gotten around to it. I think they would fit you, and you are welcome to them. My mother told me that the third child will be the smallest and have the lightest eyes. She was so right. My boys both grew to be six feet four inches, even taller than their father. Liz towers over me at just under six feet—kind of like you. But Alicia is short like me and like my mother." Maria grinned. "My mother didn't tell me that the third child often has the worst temper of the lot. Maybe she was saving me from worry."

"Thank you," Cassie said. "Alicia seems pretty calm to me."

"Wait until you get to know her better," Maria said with a chuckle.

Cassie took a deep breath and let it out slowly. "Y'all don't know me or my past, and Cecil, the man I'm on the run from, says I stole from him. I want you to know that I didn't take one thing from that horrible man. What I took was my grandmother's wedding rings and they belonged to me. I pawned them for the money for a bus ticket. I'm not a thief, and I would never repay your kindness by stealing from you."

Maria reached across the distance separating them and laid a hand on Cassie's arm. "I am a fairly good judge of character, and I believe you."

"That means the world to me," Cassie said.

"I just wanted to let you know that whatever is in the closet or dresser drawers is yours to use. Now, I'll get on out of here. Towels are under the counter in the bathroom, and there's a laundry basket in the closet. Laundry room is just off the kitchen, and everyone is responsible to take care of their own." Maria stood up and waved over her shoulder as she left.

Cassie's curiosity got the best of her, so she left the balcony and went back into the bedroom. She opened one of the two doors on the right side of the room and found a bathroom with a deep tub, a vanity with a cute little wrought-iron stool in front of it, and sure enough, the cabinet below the sink held big fluffy pink towels.

"Sweet Jesus, Mama!" she whispered. "I asked for help, not magic."

Never look a gift horse in the mouth, her mother's words came back her.

Cassie picked up a bottle of bath salts, opened the lid, and smelled them. Maria had offered her the use of anything in the room, so she promised herself a long soak that night—with maybe even some of the bubble bath she noticed on the vanity. For now, though, she eased the door shut.

"What's behind door number two?" she asked as she opened that one to find a walk-in closet. Even though several items—jeans, T-shirts, and a couple of dresses—hung on the racks, it still looked empty. Cowboy boots and two pairs of sandals were on one of the shelves, but Cassie could tell by looking at them that they were too big.

She was still standing in the closet when she heard a gentle knock on the door, and then Ted's voice. "Cassie, is it all right if I come in?"

"Sure," she answered as she crossed the room and opened the door. "Is it time for us to go buy scrubs? How far is the store from here? We sure couldn't buy much in Maryneal. We had to drive twenty miles to Sweetwater."

"It's about thirty miles to Duncan where they have a uniform shop, and yes, we really should leave now if we're going to be back by lunch," Ted answered. "I see you've been out on the balcony."

"It's lovely out there." She picked up her purse. The only

other time she had ever had two hundred dollars of her own money was when she graduated from high school. The folks at the diner where Deana still worked at that time had taken up a collection for her. She and Deana had gone shopping and used the money to buy jeans, shoes, and a couple of shirts. Cassie had been wearing a pair of those jeans, the shoes, and one of the shirts all this time later because they were still her best.

"How long does it take to drive to Duncan?" She hated to leave the room behind, but she followed Ted out into the hallway.

"Maybe forty minutes. We could go to Bowie to Walmart, and that's only thirty minutes or so, but there's a uniform shop in Duncan and they'll have the right ones for tall women," Ted answered. "Liz worked one summer for Uncle Brock and that's where she got her scrubs."

Cassie followed him down the stairs, and when they were outside, there was only one truck in the driveway. "Where is everyone?"

"Brock and Maggie have gone to the airport. Remember, they said they were going to see their daughter? Mama is volunteering at the hospital this morning. Alicia is off with her boyfriend, Daniel, and Dad is out on an errand," Ted explained as he headed straight for his vehicle.

"We're taking your new truck, then?" she asked.

"Yes, Dad took the old one out to a little place called Oscar. The oil-field equipment that was in the back is needed out there," Ted answered. "We usually just use it for a work truck."

He opened the passenger door for her and made sure she had her seat belt fastened before he closed it. Today, he wore starched and creased jeans, a leather bomber jacket over a western shirt, and black boots polished to a shine. Yesterday, he had looked more like a dirt farmer, but now he was a sexy cowboy that any woman would take a second look at.

I'm legally married to this man, Cassie thought.

Not for long, the annoying voice in her head said.

No, but I am today. Maybe sometime in the future, if someone comes along as kind and as sweet as he is, I might rethink my decision to never get married.

"Penny for your thoughts." Ted drove down the lane and turned back to the west.

Cassie felt heat rising from her neck and circling around to her cheeks. There was nothing she could do about it but look out the side window with hopes that he didn't see her blushing. "I still can't believe your folks have been so nice to me." She did not lie, but she did beat around the bush, as her mother used to say.

"My folks are amazing people, and Mama truly believes that sometimes we entertain angels by taking in strangers." A faint smile tickled the corners of Ted's mouth. "You reckon you're an angel?"

"Do you see a halo floating above my head or wings sprouting out from my denim jacket?" she asked.

Ted chuckled and then laughed out loud. "You're funny, Cassie O'Malley."

And you are laughing, she thought. *I bet your mama would sell the farm to hear that laughter.*

"Been accused of a lot of things, but never funny. Maybe you and I bring out a different side in each other," Cassie said.

"I believe we just might," Ted agreed.

"What's that painting on the side of the building?" She pointed when Ted braked at a stop sign in town.

"It's a depiction of the old Chisholm Trail," Ted answered.

"We read about that in history class," Cassie said. "I imagined myself as a girl during that time. The Civil War was just over, and the menfolk had been gone for years, then came home to round up cattle and be gone again. I don't imagine that made for good relationships."

"Think those married couples might have had some fights, do you?" Ted asked.

"Oh, yeah!" She nodded. "I would have thrown a fit if I'd been the wife back then. I would have held down the farm, milked cows, tilled the ground, and done everything inside the house and outside it too. Now the husband wants to drive cattle all the way to Kansas? That's enough to consider divorce—or maybe murder."

"You are a deep thinker, and pretty damn sassy," Ted said. "Maybe it's a good thing you weren't born at that time in history."

"Yes, it was. I would have been gathering up all the women in the area and forming a women's rights group," she said. "What about you? Do you wish you had been born at a different time?"

Ted made a right turn and drove north. "Maybe. Things might be different if there were no fast-moving trucks."

Cassie had no doubt that he was talking about his brother's wreck, but she didn't pressure for more details. "As a little girl I used to dream of being a princess and living in a castle," she admitted. "But my castle was make-believe. It had running water, pink walls, and pretty things inside. When I saw pictures of real castles, I was glad I wasn't a princess in those days."

"Reality can be an eye-opener." Ted nodded. "There was

a time when I wanted to be Wyatt Earp or Davy Crockett, but when I figured out that they had to draw water from a well or a creek, I changed my mind."

"You got to be the cowboy and wear the hat. I was on the way to trading in my princess crown for a nurse's cap. I will get it someday," she vowed as they passed by a WELCOME TO WAURIKA sign.

"I hope you do," Ted said.

Cassie watched the countryside speed past her at seventy miles an hour. This part of the world was different from the flat land where she'd lived her whole life. Here there were rolling hills and lots of trees. She even saw thickets of wild plums covered in white blooms and thought about how Deana would have squealed at seeing the possibility of so much jam in the summer.

Finally, they came into what looked like a large town, and there was the sign saying they had entered the Duncan city limits. After stopping at a couple of traffic lights, Ted turned down a street and then nosed his truck into a parking place.

"We're here," he told her. "You should buy three sets."

"Why?" she asked.

"Because you'll want to carry one in your backpack in

case a little kid upchucks on you during the day, and you'll need to wear one, wash it that night, and have the third one to wear the next day," he explained.

"Are you coming inside with me?" she asked.

"Nope," he answered.

"Why not?"

"I don't need a uniform. I'm not going to work for Uncle Brock," he said. "While you're doing whatever a nurse's aide does in the clinic, I'll be working cattle."

"I thought you said you were a farmer." Cassie frowned.

"I'm also a rancher, and it's time to work the calves that were born the past two months," Ted told her. "Farmers have to diversify to make a living."

"Is there a reason you don't want to come inside with me?" she asked.

"Yep," Ted answered.

"Want to tell me what it is, so I'm not walking into a hornet's nest of some kind?"

Ted's face turned a faint shade of pink. "The lady who owns the store doesn't like me."

"Why?" Cassie pressed.

"I went out with her daughter two times, and then I broke up with her," Ted answered. "Her name is Lydia and she wanted to get serious real fast. I didn't, and I was just trying to please Mama by dating someone."

"I see." Cassie opened the truck door. "Thanks for the heads-up."

"Sure thing." Ted tipped his cowboy hat toward her.

———————

"May I help you?" A small lady who looked like she put her makeup on with a putty knife came from behind the counter. "I'm Wilma. Are you looking for something in particular?"

"Yes, ma'am," Cassie said. "I need to buy three sets of pink scrubs. I'm not sure what size I need."

"At the back, on the round rack. Dressing room is over there." Wilma pointed toward the left and then to her right. "I'd say you might be a size six."

Cassie made her way to the racks and picked up a pair of size six tall pink scrubs and one with a size eight tag. It had been three years since she'd tried on clothing, and she couldn't even remember what size she had bought for her clinicals at vo-tech. They were blue—she did remember that.

Once she was in the dressing room, she took off her

clothes and tried on the size eight first. She couldn't believe her reflection in the mirror. She looked like a broomstick that had been shoved down into a pink gunnysack. She'd always been on the slim side like her mother, but she hadn't realized just how much weight she had lost.

She was taking the pants off when she heard the bell above the door jingle and wondered if maybe Ted had changed his mind about coming into the store. Wilma and the customer must have thought that she couldn't hear them, but everything they said came through the vent at the bottom of the door.

"I just came from the beauty shop, and you won't believe what I heard, Wilma," the customer said.

"That Ted Wellman got married yesterday, and no one even knew he was dating? I already heard that, Patsy," Wilma answered and then lowered her voice a little. "I think his new wife is in the dressing room right now. She's skinny as a rail and buying scrubs, so she's either a doctor or a nurse. Didn't you see him out there in his truck?"

Cassie backed up and sat down in the folding chair.

"No, I wasn't looking, but why would she be in here? You really think she's in the medical field?" Patsy asked.

"Why else would she be buying scrubs? She ain't much

to look at. Kinda plain and you couldn't put a dime on her face and not cover a hundred freckles," Wilma said. "Those Wellman men are supposed to be smart, but Ted kind of got left out. She might be the best he could do."

"It's not his fault," Patsy said. "He's been a bit strange since he lost his twin brother."

"That's what I told my daughter when he broke up with her." Wilma sighed. "He might have gotten this one pregnant and had to marry her. I bet his mama is fit to be tied."

Cassie was livid. How dare people gossip about Ted Wellman! He had saved her life. No one—*no one*—was going to say anything bad about him or his family.

"Probably so," Patsy said. "Just be glad that he broke up with your girl."

"Oh, I am. She thought she had caught a big fish, but I'm glad it didn't work out now," Wilma told her.

Cassie removed the scrubs and tried on the next size smaller. They fit much better, and the pants were still long enough. She went back to the rack and found two more pair like that one and took them to the counter.

"You just getting started somewhere?" Wilma asked.

"Yes, ma'am," Cassie answered.

"At the hospital here in town?" Patsy asked.

"No, ma'am, for Dr. Brock Wellman in Ryan as a nurse's aide," Cassie answered.

"I thought that was Ted's truck out there," Patsy said.

"Yes, ma'am, it is," Cassie said.

"Cash or credit card?" Wilma asked.

"Cash." Cassie pulled the bills Brock had given her from her purse.

"Seventy dollars and ninety-two cents, then. Need a pair of shoes to go with them? A lot of the nurses are wearing the Crocs these days. If you're interested in pink, that color is on sale." Wilma pointed toward the shoe racks.

Sure enough the sign in front of the pink ones said they were fifty percent off through the weekend. "Got them in size six?" Cassie asked.

The woman peeked out over the counter and looked down at Cassie's feet. "I would have put you in a nine or ten as tall as you are, and we're out of that size, but there are at least two pair of your size left."

"Only thing small about me is my feet and hands." Cassie smiled. "I'll take the shoes too."

"That'll be another twenty-five dollars and forty-two cents." Wilma cocked her head to one side.

"That wedding ring looks new," Patsy said.

"Yes, ma'am, it is," Cassie told her. "Just got it yesterday."

"Who's the lucky groom?" Wilma made change and handed it to Cassie.

Cassie slipped it into her purse, picked up the bag with the shoes and the scrubs, and smiled. "Thank you so much. Have a nice day."

"Are you the one that married Ted Wellman?" Patsy asked.

"Yes, ma'am, I am the skinny girl from Texas he married yesterday. The one with all the freckles." Cassie raised her voice. "I heard everything you said about me, and about Ted, who happens to be the most honorable and smartest man I've ever met."

With an icy glare that would have frozen off Lucifer's horns on a hot July day in Hell, Cassie walked out the front door.

She hopped into Ted's white pickup truck, slid across the seat, put her arms around Ted's neck, and pulled his mouth down to hers for a long, passionate kiss.

"What's that all about?" he asked when the kiss ended.

"Oh, I don't know," Cassie said. "Let's just say you're a whole lot nicer than some people around here. And smarter, too, since you married me."

Chapter 5

CASSIE'S GREEN EYES WERE OPEN AT 5:00 A.M. JUST LIKE always, and she hopped out of bed, ready for her favorite time of the day. She slipped into a pair of faded jeans, pulled on a pair of socks, and put on a bra and T-shirt. She hummed all the way to the kitchen where Maria already had a pot of coffee brewing. She'd lived in the house for a week and had dreamed the night before about the day she would have to leave. In her dream, she had cried so hard that she lost her breath, but her tears hadn't affected Ted one bit as he drove her to the bus station in Duncan.

"Good morning, Cassie." Maria stirred biscuit dough in a large crockery bowl. "Never seen anyone wake up so full of energy and with such a beautiful smile. You're a ray of sunshine even before the sun comes up."

"Thank you." Cassie beamed. She took a stack of plates to the table. "How many this morning?"

"Brock is delivering a baby at the hospital. Maggie is with him, so they won't be here. Ash is on the way. That makes six of us at the table." Maria dumped the dough onto a floured board, kneaded it a few times, and began pinching off perfectly uniform biscuits. She put them on a baking sheet one by one and slid it into the preheated oven.

Cassie opened the cabinet drawer where the flatware was kept and counted out forks, knives, and spoons. She pulled sunshine-yellow place mats out of another drawer. Maria had told her that first day that breakfast was the time to set the mood for the whole day—yellow brightened the table, good food satisfied the appetite, and a loving family made the heart smile.

"Why do Ash and Maggie drive over here for breakfast?" she asked. "They must have to get up awfully early."

"Maggie can't cook." Maria's eyes twinkled.

"Really?"

"No, I was teasing you," Maria said. "Maggie's a fine cook. It wasn't until the accident that took John from us that they started to have breakfast with us. It was to help all of us get through the days at first. We needed to be together. We just kept up the habit of having breakfast together as often as we could."

Cassie put the place mats and silverware on the table, then went back for plates.

"Ted told me that you once said if you are going to understand today, then you must know yesterday. So, I will begin with yesterday," Maria finally said.

Cassie watched Maria take the golden-brown biscuits out of the oven and set them on top of the stove and then crack eggs into a cast-iron skillet sizzling with melted butter.

"Eleven months after Clayton and I married, we had Liz, and then eleven months after that we had the twins, John and Ted," Maria said. "Three babies all at once was a handful, and they were barely out of diapers when I had Alicia. Some days I thought I would lose my mind, but they finally grew up."

"I can't even imagine having four kids in, what...three years?" Cassie wondered where this story was going.

"Ted and John were so close we often wondered if it took both of them to make one son. They took their first steps on the same day. They said the same first words on the same day. They laughed together, and when one of them got hurt, they both cried. When they were older, they worked for their father and saved their money until they could buy a truck to share. The accident happened when they were sixteen, but to Ted, it is still as if it happened yesterday. He has never grieved or moved on—until now."

"He hasn't shown signs of grief to me," Cassie said.

"We see them even if they are subtle," Maria told her and then went on. "John was the daredevil of the two. The first night they had their truck, they went to town in it. One of the boys from Waurika dared John to race him, to see who had the fastest truck. John did not back down from a challenge. We aren't sure what happened, but John lost control. Maybe he hit a patch of gravel. Maybe he swerved to avoid hitting a cat."

Cassie thought of the black cat that had crossed the road when she and Ted were on the way to the justice of the peace to get married. Was that bit of bad luck just waiting to happen, even yet?

"John was killed instantly"—Maria's voice cracked—"and Ted blamed himself for not forcing his brother to back down from the dare. When Ted came home he didn't say a word, and he didn't cry. One half of him seemed to be gone forever."

"Oh, my God…" Cassie's voice quavered.

Maria wiped her tears with a corner of her apron. "A mother is never prepared to lose a child. We know that we will someday lose our parents, and we are able to grieve for them when they are gone. But to lose a child is unnatural, and the grief is unnatural, so it never goes away. But Ted's grief is twice as bad because his other self—his twin—is not here anymore. It is only since he brought you home that there is some life in him." She stopped as Ted came through the dining room door.

"Where's Uncle Brock?" Ted asked. "He always beats me to the breakfast table."

"Gone to the hospital to deliver a baby," Maria answered. "Call Alicia on your phone and tell her that I'm making sausage gravy. That will get her in gear. I hear Ash in the driveway now. And holler at your daddy. He's probably still reading the paper in our bedroom."

"Okay." Ted started out of the room and then poked his head back around the doorjamb to talk to Cassie. "I'll take you to work this morning since Brock isn't here for breakfast. I have to go to the lumberyard at eight thirty."

"Thank you."

"Mornin'." Alicia bounced into the room. "Where's Uncle Brock?"

"Out at the cabbage patch finding a baby," Ted said between bites of biscuit.

"Well, in about eight months he can find one for me. I'm glad most of the family is here so I can tell everyone at once that I'm pregnant. Daniel and I don't want to get married, though. We both feel like we're too young, and he's got all that schooling to be a doctor out ahead of him," Alicia announced with a smile on her face.

"You are *what*?" Clayton pushed back his chair, and all the color left his face.

"Pregnant, Daddy," she said. "You are going to get your first grandbaby."

"Where's Daniel?" Ash asked through clenched teeth. "He and I are going to have a long talk about child support. Maybe he won't be going to college after all."

"You got anything to say, Ted?" Alicia asked.

Ted shrugged. "April Fool?"

"Dammit!" Alicia plopped down in a chair. "You just ruined my best April Fool joke ever. Maybe I can pull it on…"

"You better stop right there," Ted told her, "unless you want to spend the rest of your life in a convent." •

"You're probably right." Alicia grabbed a biscuit and

stood up. "Cassie, you need a ride to work? I'm leaving for school in ten minutes."

"I should make you stay home and scrub all the baseboards in this whole house for that stunt," Maria said.

"Ah, come on, Mama." Alicia gave her mother a kiss on the forehead. "You know I'm horrible at housework, and besides, I bet you were already thinking about rocking a grandbaby."

"I'm driving Cassie this morning," Ted said.

After breakfast was finished and Cassie had helped with the cleanup, she raced upstairs, changed into a fresh set of scrubs, and pulled her hair up into a ponytail. She had just applied a little lipstick when Ted knocked on her bedroom door.

"You ready?" he called out.

She grabbed her purse and opened the door. "All ready."

"We've got to get you a cell phone so that I can just call and not have to run up and down the stairs every time I want to talk to you," he said.

"I'll buy one as soon as I repay the loan back to Brock. Right now, I can't afford one," she told him.

"I can put you on my plan for only a few dollars a month," Ted suggested as he followed her downstairs.

"You've done enough already," Cassie said.

"You're one stubborn woman," he grumbled.

"I've been accused of much worse things," she told him as she headed outside and across the lawn.

"Do you like to push my buttons?" He opened the truck door for her.

"Nope, I'm just telling it like it is," she answered. "When I can afford a phone, I'll get one. I really don't need one right now. Who would I call? Certainly not Cecil, and what friends I had in high school have moved on with their lives. If I called them, they probably wouldn't even remember me. I can use the office phone if I need to call you or your mother. In my world, I bought what I absolutely needed and couldn't do without, not what I wanted."

In Cassie's opinion, his close-knit family had protected Ted too much. Unable to express his grief, unable even to talk about it, Ted seemed to have shut down all his feelings, but they could have made him see a therapist or talk to someone about his brother. Ted had been existing, not living, since John died, but life went on. It had to.

I'm proof of that, Cassie thought as Ted drove into town and to the Ryan Medical Clinic.

"Thanks again for the ride," she said, "and I promise I will get a phone when I can afford one."

"Like I said, stubborn," Ted said.

"And I agreed with you, Mr. Wellman." She got out of the truck and slammed the door.

"Have a nice day, Mrs. Wellman," he yelled.

Chapter 6

TED HEARD THE CLOCK CHIME ONCE. THEN AN HOUR LATER, he heard it chime again. He was no closer to coming to grips with his feelings than he had been four hours earlier when he'd first laced his hands behind his head on the pillow and begun thinking. The ceiling had become a big-screen television for visuals of what had happened almost two weeks ago now, and then moving forward up until that day.

There was Cassie in those faded jeans, fear in her eyes at the bus stop in Lindsay, and then in his arms when she fainted because of hunger. The next one was of her sitting in a chair with Alicia perched on the arm beside her as the family tried to convince her to stay. Then another one of her carrying a big platter of ham and biscuits to the breakfast table. The last one was when he took her to Brock's office a week ago in her pink scrubs. Her red curly hair was neatly pulled back in a barrette, but one red curl was struggling to escape. He reached out to tuck it back into the clasp and realized that she wasn't there.

He mentally changed stations on his imaginary screen, and suddenly there was John laughing at him for losing when they got off the school bus and raced down the lane toward home. Then when the two of them had chicken pox and were miserable together. After that was a visual of the two of them having a race on two tractors to see who could plow the most land in a day. And then, tears filled Ted's eyes and spilled down his cheeks when he saw his brother lifeless and bleeding when the fire department pulled him out of that truck.

The image of Cassie came back to him, as she'd looked when she'd come flying out of the clothing store and slid across the front seat of his truck to kiss him. He balled up his fist on his right hand and slammed it into the pillow. Damn her for making him yell, making him smile, and for making him think about things again.

Ted reached over and picked up a quarter, a dime, a nickel, and a penny from the nightstand beside his bed. He smiled in the darkness and held the cool change next to his cheek. "Get us each a pulled pork sandwich, and I'll expect you to give me the change," John had said that night before the race began. Ted had gone over to the nearby barbecue wagon and ordered the food, and then heard the faint sound of the crash. Forty-one cents had been the change, and he had kept it on his nightstand ever since.

He forced his thoughts away from that night and muttered, "I should ask someone out on a date, but no, I can't. I'm married."

Was there a possibility that, deep down inside, he had *wanted* to marry Cassie? He didn't believe in love at first sight, but maybe sometimes folks who fell in love didn't even realize they were lovestruck until later on down the road when they looked back on life.

The clock chimed again, three times. His late granddaddy had told him once that everyone should just slow down, take life easy, and quit running in circles. Well, the first two recommendations weren't too difficult to follow, but controlling his mind to keep it from running in circles and coming back to Cassie all the time—that seemed to be next to impossible.

Ted had kissed more than his share of girls, but until Cassie had blazed into his life, he'd felt as if he was simply doing what was expected of him. *She* made him feel hungry for more.

His stomach rumbled, reminding him that it had been a long time since supper. He remembered seeing a double-layer chocolate cake in the kitchen. Eating was as good a way as any not to think about her or his brother.

Ted got out of bed, flipped on a light, and scrounged around in a drawer for a pair of sweatpants. He didn't bother with a shirt. No one in the house was up at this time of night anyway.

━━━━━━

Cassie tossed and turned in her sleep, dreaming that she was running, running, and going nowhere. Her feet were like lead and adrenaline raced through her veins. That awful sheriff was chasing her, gaining ground, and she felt as if her shoes were filled with concrete. She had to keep going forward because if Sheriff Bud Tucker caught her, he would send her back to Maryneal and Cecil.

"Help me…please…" she cried out.

"Cassie?" Ted whispered. "Wake up. You're having a nightmare."

"He's going to catch me. I can't run any more. I'm so tired," she whimpered.

"It's just a dream." Ted laid a hand on her shoulder.

She doubled up her fists and pounded on his chest. "Go away. Don't make me go back with Cecil. I can't live that life."

He gathered her in his arms, held her arms down, and began to rock back and forth with her in his arms. "Wake up, Cassie. Honey, it's only a dream…"

"Ted?" She opened her eyes and wiggled out of his arms. "What are you doing here? And why are you naked?"

"I'm not naked," he protested. "I just don't have on a shirt, and you were moaning in your sleep. I came in to wake you, and you tried to beat me to death. Talk to me. What were you dreaming about?"

She wiggled free of his embrace and shivered from head to toe. "I'm so sorry. I thought I was fighting with that sheriff. I was running from him and Cecil. I was going in slow motion and they were coming after me in warp speed."

"It was just a nightmare. I'm not surprised that you're still afraid." Ted reached over and pushed her damp hair back from her forehead.

"You are real? And I'm awake, and why are you in my bedroom?" she asked.

"I'm real and you are awake. I was passing by your door on the way down to the kitchen and…" He cupped her cheeks in his hands and kissed her.

She wrapped her arms around his neck and kissed him back, then realized what she had done and moved away from him.

"I'm sorry," she said. "That was a mistake."

"Not to me," Ted said. "I am on my way to the kitchen for some cake and milk. Want to go with me? It might help to put some space between the nightmare and when you shut your eyes again."

"Yes." She whipped the covers back and stood up. "Thank you for waking me."

"No problem," Ted said.

"I'll probably gain twenty pounds by the time we get an annulment, but I'm enjoying eating so much that I refuse to feel guilty. I've started writing down some of Maria's recipes to take with me when I leave. I'm really going to miss her and all of the family. I talk too much when I'm nervous, and you kissing me like that makes me nervous," she admitted.

"You kissing me in front of the uniform store and then again a minute ago kind of makes me feel the same way," he said. "And, Cassie, you don't have to be in a hurry to leave, even after we get the annulment." Ted turned on the kitchen light and went straight to the refrigerator. "Mama likes having you here, and Brock says you're doing a great job at the clinic. You are welcome to stay until you are twenty-one and get your inheritance. When is your birthday, anyway?"

"August first," Cassie answered as she took two glasses from the cabinet.

"That's only four months," Ted said. "If you like it here, you might get an apartment in Ryan and just work for Brock and live in Ryan."

"And just where would I go to nursing school?" she asked.

"You could do online classes out of Midwestern in Lawton until it was time for clinicals. That way you could work and do classes at night," he suggested.

Cassie uncovered the cake, cut two slices, and put them on plates. "That's something to think about."

Ted poured milk into the glasses she had set on the counter and carried them to the table. "You'd have friends nearby, so really do give it some thought."

"I will." She nodded.

"Changing the subject here, do you have those nightmares very often?"

"Yep, ever since my mama died, but even more since Deana passed away. They seem silly when I wake up, but they're awfully scary when I'm asleep. Do your dreams ever bother you?" she answered.

"Yes, they do, and like you say, they seem silly when I wake up," he said.

"Do you get hungry in the middle of the night very often? A nightmare seems to make me hungry. I used to go to the kitchen and make myself a jelly sandwich in the middle of the night. Deana always had leftover biscuits and plenty of jelly." She took a sip of her milk and then the first bite of the cake. "We had a milk cow, so we had milk, but as soon as Deana died, Cecil sold the cow, chickens, and the goats all on the same day. He said since he wouldn't be there to milk her or take care of them, they had to go."

"I wouldn't mind having chickens and a cow when I build my own house," Ted said.

"You are really thinking about building a house? Where will it be, and will it be like this one?" Cassie asked.

"Not as big as this," he answered. "I'm thinking of a ranch house, all on one floor with maybe four bedrooms and a big open living room, kitchen, and dining area. Maybe with a log exterior and a big porch with a swing on one end."

"Why would you need that much room?" Cassie asked.

Ted shrugged. "I might decide to have a family someday,

and I want something that I can live in for the rest of my life. If you were building a house right now, what would you want?"

"In my wildest dreams, I never thought of building a home of my own. I lived in a trailer with my mama until she died, and we rented it. Then I lived with Deana in a small two-bedroom place until…" She paused and ate a bite of cake. "You know the rest."

"But if you could?" Ted asked.

"I guess I'd want one like you're talking about," she answered. "I like the idea of a big open space for the family to gather. Think you'll ever get married for real?"

"Don't know," Ted answered. "If you'd asked me that a month ago, I would have said no, but here lately I've begun to give it some thought. It would sure make Mama happy."

"You need to think about what would make Ted happy," Cassie told him.

"I'm not real sure what that would be," Ted said.

"Well, you better figure that out before you start thinking of a real wife and a family. Right now, you probably don't even need a house of your own. You'd most likely come here to eat anyway," she said.

"Oh, I can cook if I have to. It's not all that hard. After

all, you and my mother do it every day. How difficult can it be?" Ted asked.

"That's exactly my point. You've never done it for yourself. Maybe you'd do well to spend some time in the kitchen with Maria before you build a house," Cassie advised.

"Hey, if nothing else, I can always open up a can of beans."

"Sounds wonderful. Eating beans in your great big log cabin all by yourself. How are you ever going to find a woman who'll like living that way?" she argued.

"I can manage on my own, thanks," Ted grumbled.

"Planning to be a hermit, huh?"

"Probably, until I'm about thirty-five."

"What happens when you're thirty-five?" she asked.

"I don't know. Just sounds more grown-up than twenty-one, that's all. I figure when I'm thirty-five, I'll know what I want to do and who I want to really marry and stuff like that," he finished.

"Ah. A real marriage. To a real wife, right?" Cassie asked.

"Yeah. A real wife. What's wrong with that?" Ted answered.

"What exactly is a 'real' wife, anyway?" Cassie asked.

"A real wife would want lots of kids, and she'll love them,

and she'll love me. And she'll stand on the front porch every day to wave goodbye when I go to work." Ted drank down the rest of his milk and carried his plate to the sink.

"Wait a minute." Cassie held up a palm. "First of all, why does she have to stand on the porch like a puppet and wave to you? She's going to have a hard time doing that with a baby on each hip and another on the way. What if she wants a career—and children too? Would you help?"

"I guess so," Ted said cautiously. "As much as I could. But I don't want a woman who thinks more of her damned job than me and the children."

"That won't necessarily be true," Cassie argued. "It's possible for a woman to love her husband and her children and still hold down a job. There's day care. Your mother would love to help raise a grandchild."

"I won't have my children in day care, and my mother has raised her kids and she did the best job ever, but she isn't going to raise mine too." Ted leaned against the cabinet. He didn't realize he was gritting his teeth until his jaw began to ache. *Dammit!* He had helped Cassie with her nightmare, and all she wanted to do was argue with him.

"Well." She took her plate to the sink and then stepped up so close to him that her nose wasn't six inches from his.

"That's selfish of you, Ted Wellman. This is a lovely family you have here, and you should be willing to share your kids with them."

"Don't you tell me how to raise my kids!" he growled.

"You don't even have any kids. You aren't mature enough to be a real father. Or even a real husband. You have to let the past go and move on before you can think about either one of those things, and you're not doing a lot to do that, are you? You're just wallowing in your own little special pity party."

She turned away and started toward the door.

"Don't you walk out on me," Ted said. "What makes you think you're so smart when it comes to love and marriage?"

"I know what I feel." She whipped around to glare at him. "Which is more than you can say."

"Don't be so sure of that, Cassie," Ted said. "I know what I feel about you."

She walked over to him and stood only a few inches from him. "And what's that? How does the smart Ted Wellman feel about his temporary wife?"

"That you have baggage in your past too that you have to get over, and that even with that, I like you a lot. But you're too stubborn to accept friendship, and you fight me on everything rather than just accepting what I have to offer," Ted answered.

"Maybe I want more than what you have to offer, Ted Wellman, and like I said, you've got to take some steps forward before you can give me anything—even friendship. And as far as life, I've seen more than you will ever see, so don't go getting all holier than thou on me. You're not in charge of my life—any more than that tyrant Cecil is."

"Don't compare me to that horrible man. I mean it, Cassie. Damn it all to hell, I've done a lot for you. I don't care how mad you are, don't you dare say I'm like him. Or else."

"Or else what?" she asked. "You couldn't see my point if you wanted to because whatever I say goes in one ear and out the other. There isn't anything in your hollow head to slow it down. I'm going back to bed. I'm tired of arguing with you!"

She stormed out of the kitchen.

Chapter 7

"MARIA, DO WE HAVE TO USE THE YELLOW PLACE MATS today? I don't feel so cheerful," Cassie asked.

"What has Ted done to make you angry?" Maria asked.

Cassie headed for the cabinet drawer where the mats were kept. "How did you know?"

"Only a man can make a woman angry and sad at the same time," Maria answered.

"All we do is argue," Cassie said.

"That's normal," Maria said. "You've got an unusual situation here, and you are trying to find your footing with each other, but yes, use the red place mats this morning."

"Good mornin', Mama." Ted came into the kitchen and sat down at the table. "Where's everyone?"

"Maggie is on the way, and Brock and Ash are in the

living room with your father. You just walked through there. Didn't you notice them?" Maria asked.

"Guess I haven't been sleeping so well, and I'm a little foggy this morning," he mumbled. "Red place mats, Cassie? You know that yellow is for breakfast, and we never use red. Those have been put away for years."

"I told Cassie to put red on the table this morning," his mother said. "It's time you faced your fears and moved on, Son. Call Alicia and tell her that breakfast is almost ready."

"Remember what she told us at supper? This is Saturday. She says she's sleeping until noon."

"Hey, Maria," Brock yelled from the living room. "I've got an emergency at the hospital. Gotta run, and I'm picking Maggie up on the way. Gloria will open up this morning, Cassie."

"That makes five instead of eight." Cassie removed three place mats.

"Make that four." Ash picked up a biscuit, stuffed it with eggs, and headed out the back door. "Just got a call that one of my clients at the correctional place in Waurika wants to talk this morning. See y'all later."

Cassie removed another place mat. If Maria and Clayton decided to leave, then she and Ted could have breakfast alone that morning. She vowed she wouldn't say a word to him. Not a single one, because that would just lead to another argument.

"Cassie will need a ride this morning, Ted." Maria set a platter of eggs and bacon on the table.

"I don't need the work truck," Clayton said as he picked up the basket of biscuits. "Cassie can use it today."

"Thank you." She carried a plate of hash brown potatoes to the table.

"Ted, will you say grace for us this morning?" Maria asked.

Ted bowed his head and said a short grace.

"Thank you, Son." Clayton's voice cracked.

=====

"It wasn't easy to thank God for anything," Ted muttered.

"But you did, and that's a step in the right direction." Maria passed the eggs to Clayton.

He took out a portion and gave the bowl to Ted.

Back when John was alive, his mother called on one of them to give thanks often, but after his brother died, Ted just shook his head when Maria asked him to say grace. He hadn't been to mass since then either, or gone into John's bedroom.

He had been mad at God for taking his brother, and if he never went into that room, he could convince himself that John wasn't gone—he was just in his room. Sure, it sounded lame, but it was the only way Ted could cope at first, and then it became a crutch.

The night before, he had prayed for the first time since the wreck, asking God to please take the burden from his shoulders. All he got for an answer was a voice in his head saying, *That's your job, son, not mine. You've got all the help you need to get the job done.*

Nothing had changed in his life, except Cassie. He glanced across the table at her usual spot beside his mother. Was she sent by God Himself to help him shove the burden off his shoulders? If so, then why couldn't the good Lord have sent someone a lot less argumentative?

Clayton's phone rang, and he pulled it out of his hip pocket. "Hello, Amos, what's up this morning?" A pause and then, "Uh-huh. We'll get right on it," and he put the phone back in his pocket. "Guess I'm going to have to use the old truck after all. Amos needs some parts picked up for one of the wells up in Waurika," Clayton said. "You've got cattle to work, Son, so I'll drive up there with the parts."

"I'll drive Cassie in to work, then," Maria said.

Ted fished his truck keys from his pocket and shoved them across the table. "No need for that, Mama. She can take my truck. I won't need it today."

"That's sweet of you." Maria smiled.

"Thank you, but..." Cassie said.

Maria laid a hand on Cassie's shoulder. "No buts. You do have a driver's license, right?"

"Yes, ma'am," Cassie answered.

"Then you'll be taking Ted's truck to work today. Now would you please pass those pancakes?" Maria said.

"I've just got one question," Clayton asked. "Are you insured on any vehicle anywhere?"

"Probably not," Cassie answered. "I was insured on Deana's policy, but I'm sure Cecil has taken my name off the policy since he sold her car."

"Then Ted, you better drive Cassie to work before you start on the cattle," Clayton said, "just to be on the safe side."

"I can do that." Ted nodded. "My work crew can get started without me."

"It seems like all I do is say thank you," Cassie said.

When she slid the keys back across the table, her eyes locked with Ted's, and his pulse jacked up a notch or two.

Maybe if she stayed in Ryan and got her own apartment at the end of summer, they could at least be friends.

Are you sure that's all you want? For the first time John's voice popped into his head and startled him so badly that he blinked and glanced over his shoulder. *Come on, Brother. Look at that woman. She's beautiful and smart and independent, and you're dragging your feet. When she moves out and y'all aren't married anymore, every bachelor in Ryan will be bringing flowers to her front door.*

Ted stole a few sideways glances across the table at her. John was right. She was beautiful and smart. Plus she was downright sassy and independent. Could all those things be what was helping him move on?

I can't do it, Brother. I can't leave you behind, he thought as he finished his breakfast.

You won't ever leave me behind, but you can't wear me like an anchor tied to your butt. Live enough life for both of us, John told him.

"I'll try," Ted muttered.

"What did you say?" Cassie asked.

"I was talking to myself." Ted managed a smile. "See you out on the porch at eight fifteen?"

"I'll be there." She smiled back at him.

Cassie was ready, and no one was in the living area when she made her way downstairs. She stepped out onto the porch and breathed in the smell of roses. Everything was so peaceful that she couldn't believe what had happened just a couple of weeks before.

"Hey." Alicia opened the door and poked her head out. "Where's Brock?"

"Emergency," Cassie answered.

"Need a ride to work?" She yawned.

"No, Ted is taking me, but I think I'll just walk. I can make it before the clinic opens. Tell him when he comes down that I've left," Cassie said as she stepped off the porch and headed down the lane.

She walked up the lane, enjoying every minute of the sounds of the birds and the smell of the fresh morning air. She was stepping out on the paved road going toward town when she heard the sound of a truck's engine on the gravel. She turned to see Ted's truck throwing a spray of dust behind it. When it came to a screeching stop, gravel flew out against the trees lining the lane.

Ted rolled down the window and said, "I told you I would take you to work. You can't walk that far on a highway."

"This isn't a highway, it's Washington Street," she snapped at him, "and you don't own me, Ted Wellman. I can do whatever I want, and this morning I want to walk to work."

"When you are out this far, it turns into Highway 32," he informed her. "Are you still mad at me over the argument we had about building a house?"

"No, I just wanted to walk and clear my head," she answered. "Go on back to the house and work your cattle. I'm not helpless. I've got two legs that haven't been getting enough exercise, and I *am* walking."

"And have Mama yell at me for not taking you?" Ted asked. "No thank you."

"Are you saying I'm causing trouble between you and your family?" Cassie asked.

"If you continue to walk, you could be," he answered.

"Then so be it," Cassie said. "I'm tired of depending on someone to take me and bring me home."

"Well, darlin'," he dragged out the endearment into several syllables, "I'm driving you to work if I have to hog-tie you and deliver you over my shoulder like a sack of cattle feed. Mama told me to get over myself and move on. You told me the same thing. The two of you even had red place mats on the table this morning, and she knows that red reminds me of my brother covered in blood."

"That's your problem," Cassie said.

"Okay, you asked for it." He got out of his truck and grabbed a length of rope from the back seat.

"You wouldn't dare." She glared at him for a minute, then turned around and started walking again. After fighting with him, she would have to walk fast or she would be late, so she added a little speed. She might look like the wrath of God when she made it to the clinic but she was not getting into that truck. It was a matter of pride now, and she intended to win.

Ted's rope floated out of the air like a halo and lassoed her, pinning her arms to her sides. Before she could take another step, think another thought, or even say a cuss word, he had looped it around her three times and tied it in a knot. He threw her over his shoulder.

"Put me down right now," she demanded.

"I told you I was taking you to work," he said as he opened the passenger side of the truck and plopped Cassie down on the front seat.

"Untie me," she yelled at him. "I will go peacefully if you'll just take this rope away."

"I'm not taking any chances. There's a couple of stop signs between here and there, and you might jump out just to prove a point," he told her.

"You are evil and mean, and I don't like you." If his folks wanted emotion from him, well then, she had just given them a bushel basket full.

"You are stubborn, willful, and sometimes I don't like you either," he informed her, but he did not untie her.

A few minutes later he parked the pickup in front of the clinic, took his time walking around the truck, opened the passenger door slowly, and scooped Cassie up like she was a bride—like he had done that night at the motel after they'd gotten married.

"You put me down right now and untie me," she fumed.

"I'll put you down inside the clinic, just like I said I'd do," Ted said without a hint of a smile on his sexy face.

He managed to open the door, carry Cassie inside, and set her down in the lobby in front of Gloria, the receptionist, whose eyes were the size of saucers.

To add insult to injury, that same nasty woman—Patsy—who had gossiped about the Wellmans in the uniform shop was sitting in the waiting room.

Ted untied Cassie, held her arms down to her sides so she

couldn't slap him, and before she could say a word, he tipped up her chin and kissed her.

She was stunned speechless at the kiss, but more so that she had wrapped her arms around him and kissed him back. Even as she was enjoying the kiss, she told herself it was just to show Patsy that they were settling a lovers' quarrel.

"Have a good day, Mrs. Wellman," he said as he walked out of the clinic with the rope draped over his shoulder.

"Well, well, well." Gloria giggled. "That's a story we'll have to talk about over lunch."

Cassie could hear him whistling all the way to his truck. Add another item to that bushel of emotions, she thought as she put her purse away.

"So?" Gloria asked. "I'll treat for the story."

"You buy. I'll talk," Cassie told her.

Chapter 8

TED SAT DOWN TO A WARMED-OVER MEAL SERVED UP ON A red place mat with a red napkin under his silverware. He still hated red, might always hate it, but he didn't say a word. He just dug into his chicken-fried steak like red was his favorite color.

"Hey." Alicia brought a glass of sweet tea to the table and sat down across from him. "I heard that you hog-tied Cassie this morning, and then kissed her in the clinic."

"Gossip travels faster than the speed of light," Ted grumbled.

"When it involves something like that, it does," Alicia said. "I wish I could have seen that. What did you feel when you kissed her?"

"Why would you ask that?" Ted asked.

"She's your wife, at least for now." She reached across and stole a piece of fried okra from his plate. "But I want to know if you're thinking about making it real. Did your toes curl up when you kissed her? Did you want to drag her off to an exam room and make out with her for a couple of hours?"

"That would be my business, not yours," Ted told her, "and leave my okra alone."

"You mean this okra?" She reached over and snatched another piece. "Since you won't tell me how you felt, then I get to steal your food."

"Okay! Okay!" Ted said. "It felt right and good."

"That's all I wanted to know." Alicia grinned and yelled, "Hey, Mama, it's the truth. He did kiss her right there in the clinic. It's not just rumors."

And you thought red place mats were the worst thing that happened to you today. John's voice was back in his head. *You're doing good, Brother. One baby step forward at a time.*

Cassie helped Maria, worked at the clinic, and read a romance novel in her room that evening. She didn't mind the rumors or the fact that he'd tied her up. But it was that kiss and the effect it had on her that she needed time to process.

By the time she finished the book, she was tired of happily-ever-after. Sure, it gave her hope for her own life, and the characters had to overcome obstacles. But the heroine in the book had not been hog-tied and taken to work slung over the shoulder of her husband.

Husband!

Was that really what Ted was? That kiss said that she wanted more than a make-believe husband. Could she be satisfied with the two of them being friends when she moved out on her own?

Just friends.

That might be the best she could ever have. But the thought of looking into his eyes, like she did so often at breakfast, and seeing the miracle and dream she couldn't have made her wonder if that would be enough. She might not have a choice in the matter. He'd said he was trying to move on, but Cassie didn't want half a man, or half a twin as the case was. If she couldn't have a whole one, then she would just take the money she had saved and move out to Lawton where she could go to school on campus for her nursing degree.

"Hey." Alicia eased the door open. "Mind if I come in?"

"Not at all," Cassie said. "I was about to go out on the balcony. Want to sit out there for a while?"

"Sure." Alicia padded barefoot across the room and opened the door. "I've solved a lot of problems sitting outside and looking out over the land."

Cassie sat down in one of the chairs. "What kind of problems would you have? You have the best family and the best life."

"Money or the lack of it doesn't always define problems," Alicia said. "Did you ever wonder if it was time to sleep with a boy? Did it matter if you were poor or rich? Did you have trouble figuring out what you wanted to do with your life?"

"I get your point," Cassie answered. "And yes, no, and yes."

"Want to elaborate?" Alicia asked.

"I was fifteen when I had sex for the first time. My mother died the next week, and I thought God was punishing me for having sex without marriage. I went to confession because I had to get it off my chest, but it didn't help. I still felt guilty. I didn't sleep with another boy until I was a senior. He asked me to marry him, and I said yes, but I was only seventeen, and Deana was kind of my legal guardian. Cecil told her not to sign for me, and the guy enlisted in the army. Last I heard he married a girl from Germany and they had a baby," Cassie answered.

"Daniel and I've been sexually active for a year. He wants me to marry him when we get the first leg of our education done. He wants to be a doctor like Uncle Brock. I want to study psychology. I want to figure out how to help people get over horrible grief like Ted has trouble with. But another part of me wants to do what Liz and Justin did—get married soon, maybe at Christmas—and grow up together," Alicia said. "Ted has feelings for you."

"Where did that come from?" Cassie asked.

"He said he liked it when y'all kissed in the clinic," Alicia said.

"He's been talking about me?" Cassie wasn't sure if she was angry or maybe just a little happy about that.

"I backed him into a corner. He didn't have a choice but to answer my questions, kind of like I just did you." Alicia smiled. "So, how did the kiss make you feel?"

"Weak in the knees, but that's just a physical reaction. It doesn't mean"—Cassie picked up the romance book and showed it to Alicia—"that we're running toward a happily-ever-after."

"Hey, I read that book," Alicia said. "And that couple had to jump through fire hoops and practically dive off cliffs to get to the end. Don't shortchange what fate threw in your lap. It could be that these days, hog-tying you is just the hoops and cliffs for y'all," Alicia told her.

"I think you've been reading too many of these books." Cassie grinned.

"Probably, but they're such good examples of studying people's emotions, aren't they?" Alicia said as she headed for the door. "You might as well go talk to my brother. He's too stubborn to make the first move."

"So am I," Cassie whispered.

It was a glorious Sunday, not too hot, not too cold, but one of those just-right days that gave folks a dose of spring fever. Ted's late granddaddy had always told him that spring fever made old men think of seed potatoes and onion plants, and made young men dream of love. He had also said the hot summer sun burning out the desires of both ages was the only cure for spring fever.

Ted had dressed in starched jeans, a plaid shirt, and his Sunday boots that hadn't seen wear in several years, and was waiting in the living room when his mother and father came downstairs to go to mass that morning.

"Are you going with us?" Maria's eyes widened.

"Thought I might," he said.

"Sorry, I'm late." Cassie stopped in her tracks when she saw Ted. "Are you going to mass this morning?"

"I am," Ted said. "What's the big deal? I was raised in the church."

"But you haven't been in more than four years," Clayton said.

"I guess it's time for confession then, isn't it? Thought I'd better attend a couple of Sundays before I talk to the father." Ted shrugged.

"Well, you both look nice today," Maria said, "but we'd better get going so we aren't late. You kids can ride with us."

Ted stood up and shook the legs of his jeans down over his boots. "I'll buy lunch, then."

"That sounds fair." Clayton nodded. "I imagine Ash and Brock and Maggie will be joining us."

"Where's Alicia?" Ted asked.

"She's going to mass with Daniel today in Bowie," Maria said as she settled into the passenger seat of the truck.

Ted opened the door for Cassie and stood to one side. She wore a cute sundress and carried a lace mantle that she would put over her head when they went into the sanctuary. "Was Deana Catholic?"

"Deana was Baptist, but we only went on Easter and some-times for the Christmas ceremonies," Cassie said as she fastened her seat belt. "She wasn't really religious. Not like Mama was."

See, she's even of our faith. John was back in Ted's head.

Ted had been taught that mass simply meant gathering, and he didn't realize how much he'd missed the peace of gathering with others who appreciated coming together. He dipped his fingers in the holy water, made the sign of the cross, and then genuflected before moving on down the aisle to sit with his family in their usual pew.

Like riding a bicycle, he thought as he stood for the procession and watched Father Patrick take his place and say, "The Lord be with you."

He and Cassie, along with the rest of the congregation, said, "And with your Spirit."

When Mass was over and they were all outside the church, Ash gave Ted a hug and whispered, "I'm so glad to see you back in church."

"I'm glad to be here," Ted told him. "Didn't know how much I missed it until last night."

"Something happen?" Ash asked.

"Not last night, but I prayed for the first time since…" Ted stumbled over the words. "Since we lost John."

"That have something to do with roping Cassie and kissing her?" Ash asked in a low voice. "You do realize you've got a perfect opportunity here. You are married, so no other self-respecting cowboy is going to move in on your territory. But as soon as this annulment comes through, someone is going to ask her out, and you'll be left in the cold wishing you had taken advantage of the situation."

"I don't even *like* her most of the time. She drives me crazy, and yet..."

"And yet you're falling hard for her because she's bringing you out of your shell and putting life back in you, right?"

"Pretty much, but I'm fairly sure she doesn't feel the same about me. I don't want to make a fool out of myself," Ted said.

"She sure does have spirit. That's why we all like her so much." Ash chuckled.

"She'd be a handful to live with forever, amen," Ted whispered.

"But there would never be a dull moment, would there?" Ash clamped a hand on his shoulder. "Here comes Maggie. I hear you are treating all of us to Sunday dinner today."

"Yep, and if we hurry, we can beat the rest of the churches and not have to wait in line." Ted headed toward his dad's truck. "We're going to the fish place out west of town. I called ahead and got reservations."

That was enough about the way he felt toward Cassie for one day. Just having her sit close enough to him in the pew that their shoulders were touching had sent his pulse into double time. He stumbled over the responses because he kept thinking about that kiss in the clinic.

As luck would have it, the waitress had misunderstood the number of people and had saved a table for ten instead of only seven. She handed each of them a menu and hurried over to refill other customers' tea glasses. Brock sat at one end and Clayton at the other. Their wives were on one side, leaving the other side for Ash, Ted, and Cassie.

At least there was moving room, and they weren't scrunched in like they had been at church. Still, when the food came and Ted reached for the ketchup, his arm brushed against Cassie's, and sparks lit up the café like it was the Fourth of July. That made Ted think about the festivities they had at the ranch on Independence Day. Cassie wouldn't be twenty-one until after that, so she would be there to watch the fireworks with him.

Ted ordered the fish dinner, but when he'd finished everything on his plate, he hadn't tasted much of it.

When the meal was over, his folks went out to their

vehicles while he took care of the bill. Thank goodness no one else had made a big fuss about him going to mass that morning. He hoped that as he tried his best to move on, he could do it without a lot of fuss.

Clayton, Maria, and Cassie were in the truck by the time he paid the bill and went outside into the bright sunlight. Dark clouds were gathering down to the southwest, but as slowly as they appeared to be moving, he didn't figure they would hit Ryan for another hour or two.

Still, he wondered if that wasn't a sign.

Of course it is. Ted loved his brother, John, but he wished that he could have a little more control over when he popped into Ted's head. *You should make hay while the sun shines, and I'm not talking about real hay, Brother. Ask Cassie to take a Sunday afternoon ride with you. If you don't, the dark clouds will be the sign that you let a good opportunity slip right out of your hands.*

Ted didn't even bother to mentally argue with his brother. It had been a year since Ted had even been on a casual date, and even then it was just to please his mother. He wasn't so dense that he didn't realize that his family wanted him to feel something other than numbness, but it just wasn't there—not until Cassie stepped into his life.

Where are you, John? he wondered. *Can you see into the future from where you are? If she leaves, will these feelings I have for her go with her, and I'll go back to being numb?*

John didn't seem to want to answer those questions.

"It's probably not a bit of my business," Cassie said, "but has Ash ever been married? I've heard Brock and Maggie talk about their daughter who is studying biochemistry in Maine. I could have asked Gloria about Ash, but it seems like that would be prying. Maybe I am now, and if you don't want to answer, I understand."

"Uncle Ash is divorced," Ted answered, "and has been since I was about fifteen. He's got one son, who is a lawyer in California. He met a girl in college, and they're both lawyers in the same firm. They've been married for a year now, and she's from back east, New Hampshire, I think."

"Thanks for that," Cassie said.

"Ash's wife has moved out there to be near their son," Maria said. "She's also from California so it was like she was going home. They met at a conference and married, but she never could adapt to Oklahoma and Texas. Ash refused to move from here. It wasn't a nasty separation, but she did remarry a year after the divorce."

Clayton parked the truck in the circle driveway and

BRIDE FOR A DAY

yawned. "I'm having a nap. I always eat too much at the fish place, and it lies heavy on my stomach."

"I've got to call my mama for our Sunday chat," Maria said, "and then I'll join you for a nap."

"And that's the family history in a nutshell," Ted said as he opened the truck door, slid out, and then rounded the front to help his mother and Cassie out. "I'm going for a drive. Want to go with me, Cassie?"

"Better not," she said. "I need to do laundry and clean my room. Can I have a rain check?"

"Sure." Ted smiled. "Can I pencil you in for next Sunday?"

"Yep, you sure can." She smiled back at him.

Well, I struck out on that one, Brother, Ted thought. *You got any more of that great advice?*

He didn't even go into the house, but went from his dad's truck to his own, got behind the wheel, and backed out of the driveway. He turned on the radio to his favorite country music station. Lainey Wilson was singing "Things a Man Oughta Know," and even though Ted had heard the song before, he really listened to the lyrics this time. The words described him to a T. He was right on the verge of giving up and getting things wrong, and the part about letting a woman know if you loved her really struck his heart.

"Okay, John, I get the message," he said as he made a left turn and drove out of town. Cattle dotted green pastures on both sides of the road, but that afternoon he didn't even see them. He was too busy listening to music and thinking that every song on the radio was aimed straight at him.

The next song was "Better Together" by Luke Combs, and Ted nodded with every word. It had just ended when a streak of lightning zapped an old scrub oak tree off to his right, leaving it in two pieces as it fell to the earth. Ted stomped on the brakes and slung gravel against the fence posts forty feet away. Thunder sounded like it wasn't six inches over the top of his truck. In a split second, hard rain fell in sheets so thick that Ted couldn't see a foot in front of his truck.

He didn't even see the wild hog until it was right there in the middle of the road looking like it was lost. He swerved to avoid hitting it, and everything seemed to move in slow motion. The hog took off like a shot. The rain didn't let up. A bolt of lightning hit the road in a ball right in front of Ted, and then the tires dropped off into a ravine, and everything started spinning. He tried to get control, but the steering wheel had a mind of its own, leaving him powerless. Then the telephone pole was coming right at him, and he let go of the wheel and shielded his face with his arms. His last thought before the collision and everything went dark was that he should have told Cassie how he felt. Now it was forever too late.

═══════

Cassie had just put her bedsheets in the washing machine when the house phone rang.

"Hey, Cassie," Maria called from the living room, "can you get that for me? I'm still on my cell phone with my mama."

"Sure thing," Cassie said. "Wellman residence," she said. "This is Cassie."

"Are you Ted Wellman's wife?" the lady on the other end asked.

"No," Cassie said. "I mean yes, ma'am, I am his wife."

"This is Dana Wilson at the Jefferson County Hospital calling to inform you that your husband has been in a wreck. The ambulance is just pulling up outside the emergency room. We found this number in his billfold. The EMTs say that he's in and out of consciousness," the lady said.

Cassie's heart seemed to drop out onto the floor. "We'll be there in a few minutes."

"Who is it?" Maria came into the kitchen. "Good Lord,

child. You are as pale as a ghost. Was that Cecil? Did he find you?"

"No, it's Ted." She finally remembered to put the phone back on the base. "He's been in a wreck, and he's at the hospital." She couldn't get her feet to move. Maria was sobbing. Clayton came from the living room and took Maria in his arms.

"Is he…" Clayton asked.

"He's in and out of consciousness." Cassie's voice sounded hollow in her own ears. She shouldn't have argued with him so much. He'd done so much for her, and now she was too close to his family, and her heart ached for Maria and Clayton. They had already lost one son to a vehicle wreck. How would they ever hold up to losing another one?

How are you going to take it if he doesn't make it? Deana's voice was clear in her head.

Alicia came into the kitchen. "What's going on?"

"Ted's been in a wreck," Cassie said.

"Let's go," Alicia said. "I'm driving and we're taking Mama's SUV."

Clayton didn't even argue with Alicia but simply got into the passenger seat. The poor man looked like he'd aged twenty years in the time it took to go from the house to the vehicle. Maria got into the back seat with Cassie and reached across the distance to grip her hand.

"He's going to be all right," Maria kept whispering. "I can't bear to lose him."

Brock was already barking orders when they reached the hospital ten minutes later. Cassie didn't even realize she was barefoot until she hit the cold tile floor. She kept going right to the double doors leading from the waiting room back into the ER, but they were locked.

"Open them," she demanded. "That's my husband in there."

The lady at the desk hit a button, and Cassie ran through them. "Ted, where are you?"

"In the first cubicle, Cassie," Brock yelled. "He's going to be all right. Go tell Maria that he's going to live."

Cassie ran back to the waiting room and yelled from the door that Ted was alive and was going to be all right, and then she hurried back to Ted.

Brock pointed toward the curtain. "Maggie, take her out of here."

"I'm an aide. I can help. Tell me what to do," she said.

"Cassie, don't go. Stay with me." Ted groaned. "It was a wild hog."

"He's got a broken arm, and his ankle is twisted, hopefully

just a bad sprain, but I think it's got some cracked bones," Brock said. "We'll set the arm and put him in a boot. He'll be here for observation for at least a day, maybe two. We've got lots of tests to run. I'd feel better if you were out there with the family."

"No!" Ted yelled. "John said Cassie can stay with me."

"Hey," Brock yelled at a nurse. "Call down to X-Ray. He's showing signs of a concussion."

"Yes, sir," she said.

"And Cassie, you can stay," Brock said. "I'm going out to talk to Maria and Clayton and let them come see him for a few minutes."

Cassie moved over to the bed and took Ted's hand in hers. "I'm right here, and I'm not going anywhere."

Ted looked past her at the end of the bed, then he closed his eyes and muttered, "You are right, John. She's a keeper."

"I'm going to step out for just a minute," Maggie said. "If you need anything, I'll be at that desk out there."

When Cassie tried to remove her hand, Ted held on, so she pulled up a chair and sat down beside the bed. "Please don't have a brain bleed," she whispered.

His eyes popped open. "My arm hurts, Cassie. What happened to me?"

"You were in a wreck," she told him.

"Where's John? Did he make it?" he asked.

Maria had dried her eyes, and Clayton looked a lot less worried than when they'd arrived with Alicia.

"Oh, Son, what did you do?" Maria asked.

"There was a wild hog, and I swerved. Is John okay?" He frowned. "I want to see him."

"John is fine," Clayton said.

Ted sighed and then grabbed his head with his healthy arm. "I bet he's got a headache just like mine."

"You've scared the hell out of us all," Alicia snapped at him. "Why didn't you just hit the hog?"

"Hog didn't do nothing to me," Ted said and then grinned. "This is some good pain medicine. Is John getting this, too, so that he feels like he's floating?"

"Okay, folks." Brock peeked into the room. "He's going to X-Ray now, so everyone needs to clear out. I'll come get you as soon as he's back. I'm going to set his arm, and if we're lucky, he'll just need a boot on his foot for a while. He's fortunate to be alive."

Ted's eyes snapped wide open, and he slowly took in his surroundings. His mother was asleep in a chair over in the corner. Cassie's mop of red hair was fanned out on the side of his bed, and she had a firm grip on his hand.

Only his eyes moved as he scanned the whole room again. An IV bag dripped something into the bend of his arm. The other one was in a cast, and his leg, with one of those boot things on it, was elevated on a pillow. Had he fallen down the stairs or what?

Then it all came back to him in a flash. Rain was pouring down, and a wild hog was in the middle of the road. He stomped the brakes and went into a slide.

Little different from my wreck. John chuckled in his head. *But you get to live through yours, so make the most of every day.*

Maria rushed to the side of his bed. "You're awake. How are you feeling? Do you hurt anywhere?"

"If it's part of me, it hurts." Ted groaned. "Am I in a hospital? Why am I here? Take me home."

Cassie jerked her head up and let go of his hand. "Yes, you are in the hospital. You've got a mild concussion, a broken arm, and a fractured ankle, so that boot is your friend for several weeks."

"And about four stitches on your arm above the cast," Maria told him.

"How are you feeling, now that you're awake?" Cassie finger-combed her unruly curls and whipped them up into a messy bun on top of her head. "Do you remember what happened?"

"Rain and a wild hog in the middle of the road. I stomped on the brakes and lost control. John wasn't with me, was he?" Ted asked.

Maria sighed. "No, he's been gone for a while now."

"I thought he was with me," Ted whispered.

"Maybe his spirit was right there," Cassie said. "The important thing now is that you heal."

"And face reality." Ted tried to grin. "Ouch! What happened to my face? It hurts."

Cassie dug around in her purse and brought out a compact. She flipped it open and held it up so Ted could see.

"Looks like I've been in a bar fight," he muttered. "What time is it?"

"Eight in the morning. You've been here since yesterday noon. Cassie and I stayed with you all night." Maria pushed the intercom button on the side of the bed and asked the nurse to page Brock.

Brock pushed the door open and came in with a tablet in his hand. He laid it to one side and pulled a tiny flashlight from his pocket and looked into both of Ted's eyes. "All the tests we've done look good. Your eyes are better than last night. How's your memory?"

"I remember everything up until my truck started rolling. Past that, it's a fog," Ted answered.

"You don't see John at the end of the bed?" Brock asked.

"No, but I do hear him talking to me sometimes these days," Ted answered.

"Perfectly understandable. Sometimes I hear my dad fussing at me. How do you feel on a scale of one to ten? One being the worst and ten the best."

"Minus fifteen," Ted answered. "Like I was the only chicken at a coyote convention. My head hurts worse than if I had a hangover, my arm is throbbing, and my leg is killing me."

"Well, thank God." Brock laughed. "Anybody that hurts that bad can't be dead!"

———

At Brock and Maria's insistence, Cassie went home that morning. At her own insistence, she went to work at the clinic that day, but that evening Alicia drove her to the hospital. She was so tired that she fell asleep in the car on the trip and Alicia had to wake her when they arrived.

"You should have come home and gotten some rest instead of working," Alicia scolded.

"Probably, but I was too wound up to sleep," Cassie said. "I'm not sure I want to be a wife, but I know I don't want to be a widow. Plus I couldn't bear to see all of you lose him after what happened to John."

"That's sweet," Alicia said. "I'm going in with you for a few minutes, but then Daniel and I have a session with a photographer for senior pictures. Graduation is in two weeks. I sure hope Ted is able to go."

"I bet he'll be there. We'll get him one of those scooters to put his knee on. Not much is going to keep him down," Cassie said with a smile.

She and Alicia found the door to Ted's room open and discovered an aide hovering over his bed. "Y'all come on in. I was just gathering up his supper dishes. Dr. Taylor says he can go home soon as someone comes to get him. Maybe in an hour or two when we get the paperwork done. He says that he's going to teach me the two-step when he gets all better."

Lara, according to her name tag, had flowing dark hair that swung past her waist when she bent over him to straighten his pillow.

"Really?" Cassie's tone was cool.

"Which sister or cousin are you?" Lara asked. "I haven't seen a red-haired Wellman yet."

Cassie crossed the room and brushed a kiss across Ted's lips.

"I'm his wife," she said.

"Oh, really?" Lara raised her eyebrows. "I guess we won't be going to the Rusty Spur and two-stepping, then?"

"We'll have to wait until the end of the summer to see about that," Ted told her but his eyes were on Cassie.

"Call me if you still want to go then." Lara winked.

"Theodore Ashton Wellman, what's going on here?" Alicia snapped. "Have you lost your mind? Maybe you ought to stay in here for a few more days to make sure you didn't scramble your brain worse than Uncle Brock thinks you did."

"What?" Ted asked.

Alicia crossed her arms over her chest. "Now it's going to be all over the county that you were flirting with Lara Dillard. She's a gold digger, and she's got the reputation of a doorknob."

"What does that mean?" Cassie asked.

"It means that every guy in the county had a turn." Alicia shook her finger at her brother. "Folks will say that you knocked a few screws loose in that wreck to even be talking to her."

"I wasn't flirting," he protested.

"Yes, you were," Cassie told him.

Brock poked his head in the door and chuckled. "I could hear Alicia fussing at you halfway down the hall. If you can do that, then I'm sure you're ready to go home. I'm sending a scooter with you, and I suggest you sleep in the downstairs guest room. You won't be climbing stairs for a while. Alicia, are you driving him home?"

"Nope," she answered. "Daniel and I are taking sunset pictures in our caps and gowns. He can call Daddy to come get him."

"I'm glad," Ted said. "I don't want to hear her griping at me all the way to the house."

"On that note, I'm leaving," Alicia said. "I'm glad you are alive, but you can be an idiot sometimes, Brother."

"And you can be bossy all the time," he shot back and then turned to Cassie. "Get my jeans and boots, please, so I can get dressed to go home."

"We cut your jeans off you, and you won't be wearing boots for a while, except for the one that's on your foot now. I suggest you wear sweat bottoms until your ankle heals. T-shirts will stretch over the arm cast better than your chambray shirts," Brock said. "Paperwork should be in here pretty soon. Want me to call Clayton and Maria?"

"Yes, please." Ted sighed.

When Brock was gone, Ted turned to Cassie again. "What was that kiss all about?"

"Just showing Lara that you were taken," she answered. "At least until the end of summer."

"And past that? Are you really going to move away from Ryan?" Ted asked.

"One day at a time, and we'll cross that bridge when we get to it," Cassie said. "What did you have for supper?"

"I don't know what it was, but I couldn't make myself eat it. I haven't had anything but Jell-O and pudding all day. Can we please get a pizza on the way home?" he asked.

"Yes, we can." She smiled and resisted the urge to touch her lips to see if they were as warm as they still felt. "And they had to cut one of your boots off. Your leg was swollen, and they were afraid they'd damage your ankle even more if they tried to pull it off."

"Cut them off?" His voice shot up an octave. "You let them cut my custom-made boots off? They were handmade! John and I got a pair just alike for our fifteenth birthday. Some wife you are."

"I told the nurse she could throw that boot out. We'll take the good one home with us. You can build a shadow box to keep it in." Cassie's anger shot to the top. "Maybe even make a shrine in your new house for your brother since you can't get past his death."

"Damn it, woman, don't you talk to me like that," Ted growled.

"Dead men don't usually care about boots or jeans," she said through clenched teeth. "No one thought about waiting until you regained consciousness so they could ask you if they could cut off your clothes. They were all too busy trying to save your life. And I sat up with you all night, holding your hand because you got agitated when I wasn't right here. And don't call me 'woman.' That's what Cecil called Deana when he was mad at her."

Ted grabbed her hand.

"I'm sorry, Cassie. You're right. I shouldn't complain. I am alive—especially when you're around."

"Hmmph." She tried to pull her hand away from him, but he held on to it. "Apology not accepted."

"Why not?"

"Because you were flirting with Lara."

"Come here, Cassie." Ted pulled her close to him and brushed a soft kiss across her lips. "You know I don't want that nurse. I want you."

"Why?"

"Sit here beside me. You need some tender loving care too."

"Ted, you've got a broken leg and a broken arm. Providing TLC is my job, not yours."

"Well, right now it's my job," he said. "I appreciate all you've done for me. You've taught me to feel again and I'm grateful. I don't want you to leave Ryan. There, I said it."

"Why?" She sat down in a chair that was close to the bed, but he didn't let go of her hand.

"You've been good for our whole family, and I appreciate that, and I want us to be friends."

Friends!

Cassie wanted more than that and wasn't going to stick around Ryan and watch him ruin his life with someone like Lara.

"I've been thinking about a lot of things, Cassie."

"Like what?"

"Like you and me, for starters. I almost got killed. I figure I got a second chance at life here. And I don't feel like blowing it."

He was silent for a long moment.

"John never got to—" Ted struggled to speak, and his

voice was thick with emotion. "John never got to love any-body. After he died, I wasn't able to feel anything, but with you in my life, that's all turned around."

Cassie nodded and let him talk.

"The day you sat down across from me and put your hands on mine—" He stopped and looked at her. "Things began to change."

"I can see that, and it's the reason your folks didn't send me packing that first day."

Ted squeezed her hand gently. "Up to now we've done more arguing than talking. I want to change that. Getting married is no way to begin a relationship, but we know each other now, so we can start over."

"Go on," Cassie said when he paused.

"Look, this is what I'd like to try. We'll still plan on ending the marriage when you turn twenty-one and get that inheritance. Until then, please help me deal with my past, my brother's death..." Ted paused again.

"And?" Cassie asked.

"You make me feel like a whole person again. Like I came back to life. I don't ever want to lose you. I think I'm falling in love with you. I say I think, because I don't have anything to compare this feeling to. I've never been in love before."

"I think I love you, too, but—"

"Grandpa told me that are no 'buts' in real love," Ted said.

"But there are in real life," Cassie insisted. "I think I should go away after Ash gets us unhitched. Go back to school and get myself an apartment and grow up some. You need some space too. To find out if I'm the woman you really want."

"I don't need space," he said sulkily. "I need to get these casts off and throw you over my shoulder and take you away and teach you once and for all how much I love you."

"Whoa, caveman. That's not how it's going to be. These are the ground rules: You and I are married in name only. It would probably be better if we didn't even mention the word 'marriage' at all if we're really going to get to know each other. We can try not to drive each other crazy, or bicker too much. Then maybe we can talk about a relationship. But I want a divorce or an annulment first, so we can start over and do it right."

"Okay," he agreed. "Maybe we're both too young to be certain of anything, but can I get one promise from you?"

"Maybe, but I'm not promising until I hear what it is."

"You said you think you love me. Will you give me a

chance after we're divorced to show you that I really love
you?"

She nodded. "I promise."

Chapter 9

After the first day of watching reruns on television and enduring his mother's pampering, Ted was already getting cabin fever. He asked his dad if he could do some work in the office that morning.

"I would really appreciate it if you would input about a month's worth of invoices and data into the computer," Clayton said, "but you hate to do that kind of work."

"Even paperwork beats boredom, and right now Amos is having to take care of my hired hands. I can't run this damned scooter over uneven ground, and I can't maneuver crutches with one arm in a cast." Ted stood up, put his knee on the scooter, and used his left hand to guide it from the living room to the office.

He had just logged in to the computer when the house

phone rang. He reached over and picked it up from the base. "Wellmans'. This is Ted speaking."

"This is Cecil Gorman," the voice said.

Ted almost dropped the phone. "Yes, sir. What can I help you with today? Are you looking for a job or maybe interested in one of the bulls I've got for sale?"

"It's not what you can do for me, it's what I might do for you," Cecil said. "I'm on my way to your place now. We'll talk when I get there."

"About what?" Ted tried to keep calm, but it wasn't working.

"Don't play dumb with me, boy," Cecil growled. "About Cassie. You don't want me to go to the sheriff's office and bring him with me, do you? He'll put Cassie in my truck, and she'll be on her way back to my place before you can sneeze. She's a thief, and poor thing isn't right in the head. I expect you to hand her over to me, or else."

"Or else what?" Ted asked, but there was no answer. "Dammit!" he swore as he put the phone back on the base, and then picked it up again. He hit the speed-dial number for his uncle Ash.

"Wellman Law Firm," the office manager answered.

"This is Ted, and I need to talk to Ash right now. It's an

emergency." Ted didn't even recognize his own voice. While he waited for Ash to answer the call, he pulled his cell phone from his pocket and called his father.

"Daddy, where are you?" he asked.

"I'm still in the living room. What's wrong, Son?"

"Cecil Gorman just called me. He's on his way out here," Ted answered.

"Call Ash," Clayton said.

"I'm waiting for him to answer the landline," Ted said.

"I'll be waiting on the porch. After you talk to Ash, come on out there with me," Clayton said. "Don't worry, Son. We'll take care of this."

"Yes, sir," Ted said and then told Ash about Cecil's call on the landline.

By the time Cecil arrived, they were all three sitting on the porch. The man got out of his brand-new truck and swaggered across the yard as if he had all day. "Which one of you is Theodore Wellman?"

"That would be me, Mr. Gorman, and this is my father, Clayton, and my uncle Ash. I've asked him to be present since he's our family lawyer. What is it you want to talk about?"

"You know what I'm here for. I told you on the phone. My wife, may she rest in peace"—he removed his cap and bowed his head for a moment—"and I have full custody of Cassie. She's always been slow and not right in the head, but she was good to my late wife. Deana made me promise to take care of her until she was twenty-one and we could put her in a group home for people like her. I've got one located in Sweetwater where I think she'll be very happy. Now, if you'll go get her, I'm willing to drop the burglary charge."

"Cassie is very intelligent," Ted said. "She's been working for my uncle Brock as a nurse's aide for weeks now. We don't see any signs of a woman like you are describing. Evidently, you've come all the way up here for nothing because this Cassie O'Malley isn't the woman you are looking for."

"Why are you really here, Mr. Gorman?" Ash asked. "Do you have legal documents saying that Cassie is mentally challenged, or that you have legal custody of her until she is twenty-one?"

"No, but..." Cecil began to twist his hat.

"And you really expect us to just hand her over to you on your word?" Ash asked.

"I do have proof that Cassie stole some jewelry and run off, and when I tracked her down to Lindsay, the sheriff said that you had married her. I guess it's time to call him and have her arrested if you aren't going to tell her to come down here and get in this truck with me."

"Sheriff Tucker has no jurisdiction in our county." Clayton took his phone from his pocket. "But I can call the sheriff of Jefferson County and ask him to come out here and take your statement. Exactly what jewelry did she steal? We'll need a full description, and maybe a picture to prove that it even existed would be good."

"I guess it's pretty plain that we're not giving you Cassie, so it would be good for you to just go on back across the Red River," Ted said.

"I'm not leaving without her." Cecil thrust his chin up and looked down his nose at Ted.

"Like I said"—Clayton started to poke numbers into his phone—"I need a description of what she took."

"A set of wedding rings." Cecil growled.

"How much are they worth?" Ash asked.

"Who knows? She hocked them, and the pawnshop owner has to keep them for six months before they can be sold. But them rings is still stolen, and the law can come down on her for that." He shifted his eyes toward the house.

"Cassie told me they were her grandmother's rings," Ted said.

"Well, yes. They were"—Cecil nodded—"but they were

given to my wife as a little payment for us taking her in and letting her finish high school."

"We seem to be going in circles here. If we could get back to what you want—" Ash said.

"I told you already. I want Cassie back," Cecil told him.

"And if she doesn't want to go?" Ash asked.

"Don't matter a damn what she wants. She's in my care, and I'm takin' her. I didn't give my consent for you to marry her, boy." He shot a dirty look toward Ted.

"She was past eighteen and didn't need your consent," Ted informed him.

"How much?" Clayton asked.

"How much what? Do you mean money?" Cecil asked. "Are you tryin' to buy me off? I figured you'd be tired of her sass by now and glad to get rid of her. You can't actually be tellin' me you'd pay me to leave her here."

Ash and Ted exchanged a glance.

"Now why would I pay you for that?" Ted inquired. "She's not a thing to be bought and sold. Slavery was abolished a few years back, in case you hadn't heard."

Cecil's face paled. "What are you talking about—"

"I just want to know how much the rings are worth. We'll pay you back for them," Ash said.

Cecil held up a hand. "Wait a minute." He crossed his arms over his chest. "I heard at the café in town that you two are just waiting to get an annulment and that you're only hiding her out here from me. I'm not just interested in the price of those rings. I need that girl."

"We are married. And why are you so determined to take Cassie back to Texas? It wouldn't be because you sold her to some sex-trafficking folks, would it, and if you don't deliver her, they want their money back—maybe with interest that's been building every day since you didn't give her to them?"

Cecil began to fidget with his hat even more, and his eyes shifted from the house to the trucks in the driveway, but he wouldn't look at any of the men on the porch.

"That's just another one of her lies. I'm a law-abiding truck driver," Cecil protested.

"Yes, sir, and I'm Santa Claus." Clayton looked down at his phone. "Let's see what our sheriff has to say when he hears this story."

"Hey, I treated her good. I want you to know that. She never wanted for food or anything else—"

"How much?" Ash pulled his billfold from his pocket. "Two hundred dollars?"

"For the rings?" Cecil acted offended. "Those rings was worth a helluva lot more than that!"

Ash laid out another hundred on the porch rail. "That's my final offer, and it comes with a stipulation. If you ever cross the Red River bridge into Oklahoma again, I will figure out a way to put you so far back in jail that you won't see sunshine again."

Cecil reached for the cash.

"Oh, no, I want a receipt that you've been paid the full value of those rings. Cassie owes you nothing now," Clayton said. "I want this done legal with a signature."

"I ain't got a receipt," Cecil said.

"I'll get one," Clayton said. "I've got a whole book of them in my office."

In just a couple of minutes he was back and had handed the book off to Ash, who filled in the receipt and handed it to Cecil to sign.

"I should be getting more than this. I kept that girl for more'n four years. Fed her, clothed her, and gave her a room of her own," Cecil grumbled as he scribbled his name.

"And she gave up college to stay with your ailing wife. She cooked and cleaned, kept a garden, and took care of animals," Ted said.

"If we took all that into consideration, I bet a judge would make you pay *her*." Ash left the receipt in the book and handed it back to Clayton. "You might want to put that in the vault just in case you need it."

"How much did you get for her?" Ted asked.

"Five hundred up front," Cecil said, then turned scarlet and clamped a hand over his mouth. He whipped around and ran toward his truck.

Ted started to stand up, but Clayton laid a hand on his shoulder. "Let him go. I'll call our sheriff and tell him the story, and he'll put a bug in the ears of the law enforcement down in that area."

"What if I hadn't stopped for coffee," Ted whispered.

Ash clamped a hand on his other shoulder. "But you did, and now we're rid of Cecil for good. I wouldn't be surprised if he's transporting women to sell on his long hauls. How else would he know how to even sell Cassie? But now that the law is on to him, he might find himself in more trouble than he tried to bring down on Cassie."

"I hope so," Ted said. "Thank you both for being here with me."

"That's what family is for," Ash said.

"And remember, Son, Cassie is family now," Clayton told him.

"Will you please take me home for lunch?" Cassie ran from the waiting area at the clinic to Gloria's desk.

"Whoa! Hello, Cassie! Slow down. You look like you're about to faint."

"I just saw Cecil's truck go by, and he's headed toward the ranch," Cassie said.

"We close up shop from twelve to one," Gloria reminded her.

Maggie came from one of the exam rooms. "What's going on?"

"Cecil's truck just went through town," Cassie answered.

"I can go now," Maggie told her. "My car is parked out back."

Cassie grabbed her purse and ran toward the back exit. Maggie was right behind her, but when she got in the car, she said, "We have to go by the community center and pick Maria up. She and I are giving the senior girls a little dinner next week. Wellman Enterprises does this every year. The Booster Club does something for the boys. I only needed to work this morning because Brock has afternoon rounds at the hospital, so I brought Maria to town with me. I'm talking too much. Are you sure that it was Cecil's truck?"

"Yes, ma'am, positive." Cassie could hear a quaver in her

own voice. "The window was rolled down and I got a good look at him."

"Here's my cell phone." Maggie tossed it over into Cassie's lap. "Call Maria and tell her to meet us out front."

"Are you on the way already?" Maria asked when her phone rang.

"This is Cassie, not Maggie, and…" She went on to tell her what she had seen.

"I'll be on the sidewalk when you get here," Maria said. "I'm calling Clayton. We may have to hide you away somewhere else, but don't worry. There's plenty of places to do that."

Ash and Clayton were sitting on the porch when they arrived, and there was no sign of Cecil anywhere. Cassie was out of the car as soon as Maggie stopped and jogged all the way to the porch. "Did Cecil come out here? Where is he? Can he make me go back with him?"

"He didn't have a leg to stand on," Ash said. "Go on in the house. Ted is in the office. Y'all need to talk."

"Is he all right? What happened?" she heard Maria ask, and then she was tearing across the living room in a dead run.

"Ted?"

"I guess you know that Cecil was here. Ash and I got rid of him. I doubt that he'll come back."

"What did he want? Are you sure? Did he say that he would leave me alone? What about the burglary charge?" She rattled off questions so fast that they made *her* head spin.

"He wanted us to turn you over to him. He tried to tell us that you were mentally challenged, but he used coarser language. I'm sure he won't be coming back, and he will end up in jail if the authorities find out he's part of that trafficking ring, which I think he is because how else would he have the contacts to sell you to them. Forget about the burglary charge. It has been dealt with," Ted said.

Cassie crossed the room and sat down in Ted's lap. "Thank you, thank you, thank you. I can't ever repay you, but this is such a load off my mind. I've been looking over my shoulder ever since I got here."

Chapter 10

"IT'LL BE A FEW DAYS BEFORE YOU WALK EASILY," BROCK told Ted on the morning before Alicia's graduation that night. "Use your crutches for a couple of weeks, but at least you can get back out into the field and supervise your hired hands."

Ted had been dreaming of taking Cassie dancing after his boot came off and the cast on his arm, but right now he couldn't two-step any faster than an armadillo could fly.

His dad put down the magazine he'd been reading in the waiting room at the clinic and rose to help him.

"Thanks, Dad, but crutches are a little like riding a bicycle. Once you get the hang of it, you never forget. Remember when I fell out of the pecan tree and sprained my leg? This isn't a whole lot different, except this bum arm makes things a little tougher," Ted said.

He stared out the window at the passing countryside while his father drove in silence. One good thing about the Wellman men—they usually knew when to leave people alone and let them work through their problems.

That afternoon his mother and Aunt Maggie were busy decorating the house for Alicia's graduation party that evening. Their sister Liz and her husband, Justin, were coming home for the event, and the whole house was astir with energy. No one paid any attention to Ted, so he decided that it would be a good time to take care of a task that had been on his mind for the past four weeks.

He slowly made his way up the stairs for the first time since his wreck. He headed to John's room, but he couldn't make himself open the door. He just stood there, staring at the knob with something that felt like a cold chunk of ice in his gut.

Finally, after several minutes, he put his hand on the knob and peeked inside. He remembered when he had moved into a room down the hallway that had one bed in it. His mother and his sister Liz had moved all his clothing to the new room and closed the door. Everything in the room was covered with dust, but then it had been more than four years since the door had been closed.

"I'm sorry, Brother. It wasn't right to shut you up in this room and not let you go," Ted muttered.

Two twin beds were separated by a nightstand holding a dusty lamp shaped like a football. Newspaper articles about the calves they'd shown at the county fair, football games they'd played in junior high, and their favorite pinup of a movie star were all still thumbtacked to a huge bulletin board on the other side of the room. A tall chest of drawers and a double dresser sat against another wall.

A box was sitting on John's bed, and Ted eased down beside it. The pictures that had been strewn across his dresser were tucked away in the box. His mother must have planned to clean out the room at one time, but she couldn't bear to do it.

"That wasn't fair to her," he muttered as he looked through them.

She was trying to protect you. John's voice was back, stronger this time than ever. *It wasn't that she didn't love me, but she didn't want the pictures to be a constant reminder to you.*

Ted pulled out one picture after another and laid them on the bed—photos of the twins when they had first walked, when they played T-ball, when Clayton first let them drive the tractor—sixteen years of happy life in one big card-board box.

Ted picked up the last photo taken of him and John. The blinds of the room were still drawn, and it was difficult to make out their faces, but they were standing in front of a tractor. He remembered it being the end of the day after they had had a race to see who could plow the most ground in eight hours. It had been a tie. Two weeks later, John was dead.

Ted studied it for a moment and put the picture back in the box. It was time to put them all back on the dresser and put the room to rights. He needed to remember the happy times he had had with his brother, not keep John shut up in a room as if he had never lived.

Ted picked up a baseball bat and took a short swing at an imaginary ball. Last time he'd been in this room, his brother had still been very much alive.

"Am I crazy?" he asked.

No, but if you don't move on, you will be.

"Ted?" Cassie peeked into the room. "Lord, you scared me. I heard you walking around but I didn't know if it was you or a ghost in here," she said.

"This was our room before John died," he said. "I moved

out that very night, and I've never been back in here until right now."

"Can I come inside, or would you rather do this alone?"

"I would love for you to come in with me." Ted nodded. "Will you help me take care of something I should have done years ago?"

Cassie took his hand and gave it a squeeze.

"Cassie, I want to put these pictures back on the dresser. John needs to be visible, not tucked away in a box," Ted said.

"Then we're going to have to clean this room. John's memory doesn't need to live in a room that smells like stale air and dust mites. I'm glad you are ready to do this, but maybe you better set them up. I wouldn't know the order you had them in."

"Probably so," Ted said.

"But first we dust and vacuum and get rid of all the cobwebs," Cassie said.

"Kind of symbolic of all the years I've let dust accumulate on my heart," Ted said.

"Yep, it is," she said. "I can help clean the room, but the business with your heart belongs to you."

"Oh, no!" Ted told her. "I wouldn't be where I am today if you hadn't coerced me into marrying you," he teased.

"Seems like I remember it was you that came up with that brilliant idea," Cassie reminded him. She picked up a picture and studied it. "Which one is you?"

"Right there on the left. We were identical twins, but he usually outweighed me by a few pounds," Ted explained.

"That's incredible," she said and then pointed toward a newspaper clipping that was yellowed with age and curling around the edges. "I can't tell the difference here. It's like a mirror image."

"I'm the one in the blue shirt." Ted laughed. "Mama bought red for John and blue for me all the time. That's how she told us apart."

"But this is a newspaper photo. You're both in black and white." Cassie laughed too.

"I'm the one on the left...poetic, huh, since I was the left one," he said.

"Yes, you are." Cassie nodded. "And I was the one left when my mother and then Deana died. But we're alive and we're not alone anymore. They wouldn't want us to grieve for them one more day."

Ted took her in his arms and held her close for a long moment.

"Thank you, Cassie," he said. "Sometimes you know just the right words to say."

"Sometimes?" She raised an eyebrow.

"Yep." He nodded. "The other times it's just the opposite."

"Keeps you on your toes." She grinned.

"All right." Ted had to step back from her or he was going to topple both of them onto his old twin bed and kiss her until they were both breathless. With his bum leg and arm, that wouldn't be a good thing, even if in his mind it did sound wonderful.

"You sure were cute little fellows," she said. "Hey! I can tell the difference now. This one is you and this one is John."

Ted looked over her shoulder. "Not even Daddy could tell us apart when we were that young."

"Well, I can," she argued. "Your eyes are different from John's and your smile is just a little more crooked. Your eyes are softer, Ted."

He turned the picture over to check the names his mother had jotted on the back. "You're right, Cassie."

"Of course I am," she said. "In this one you tried to fool your mother, didn't you?" Cassie smiled as she studied another picture. "You and John traded shirts, huh?"

Ted had a choice: faint or fall down. Cassie was amazing. No one had ever known that he and John had traded shirts for their school pictures, and neither of them had ever confessed. This family outsider had taken one look and figured out the joke they had played on the teachers that day.

"How'd you know?" Ted asked.

"By your eyes, Ted. I'd know your eyes anywhere. Did you and John always share this room, even though you were teenagers?"

"Yes, we did." He took a very deep breath. "Let's get the dresser dusted so we can put these back."

"Don't go anywhere," she said as she ran out of the room.

Seconds later she returned with the vacuum cleaner. "I can't let you leave John in here without cleaning the room." Cassie opened the blinds. "We'll start by letting some light in here. Ted, you can always come back and visit when you want. I'll dust first, but when I start to vacuum, you have to stand out in the hall."

"Why?"

"Because if you don't, I'll have to ask you to raise your feet, and if I vacuum under them, you'll never get married," Cassie said as she pulled a dust rag from her hip pocket and went to work.

"That's crazy!"

"Oh, come on." Cassie plugged the cord in the outlet. "You've heard that old superstition. It's not that far from

Texas to Oklahoma. Granny always made me go into the other room while she vacuumed."

Ted laughed loudly, but when she turned on the vacuum, he went to the doorway, where he watched her run the sweeper over the entire room.

Never get married?

Funny.

He *was* married.

"All done." She wheeled the vacuum back out into the hallway closet where Maria stored it.

"There's one more picture, but this one doesn't go in here. It goes in the living room on the piano." He stared at it for a long time. "Liz was a teenager with a mouthful of braces, John and I had to have been about thirteen, and Alicia still had braids."

"I'll take that one downstairs and come back and strip those beds. Do you want to go back down now or later? I can help you, or you can sit in that chair over there while I get clean sheets for the beds."

"Cassie, no one will probably sleep in here, so—"

"It doesn't matter. It needs to be done," she said. "Sit or go downstairs?"

"I can't just sit and watch you work. I'll take the sheets off. Need to exercise my arm and leg anyway," he said.

"Good. I was hoping you'd stay so we can talk." She dashed off again.

Ted peeled back a bedspread and threw it on the floor.

When she returned, he threw a pillow at her. She side-stepped it and tossed the sheets over on the bare mattress. "Why did you do that? Did it have a spider in it?"

"No, I'm challenging you to a duel of pillows. The last hit wins, and the winner takes the loser to dinner tomorrow night."

"No way. I might hurt you, but I will accept your challenge for a later date, and you can take me to dinner tomorrow night," she told him.

"I win!" he declared.

"But we didn't have a pillow fight," she said.

"No, but I win anyway because you just accepted my offer for a real date," he said.

"I'm not bashful when it comes to food, so you'd better have a hefty amount of cash in your wallet," she teased.

"I'll take you to dinner on Friday and you can eat until I'm broke." Ted sat down on John's bed and pulled her down beside him. He breathed in a heady mixture of lemon furniture polish and a trace of sweet perfume. "You are so beautiful, Cassie," he whispered.

"I'm not used to getting compliments like that when I clean house."

"I want you to get used to a lifetime of it."

"What—cleaning house?" she said in mock horror.

"No, silly. Compliments."

Ted leaned forward and nuzzled her neck. His mouth touched hers and she closed her eyes, ready for a kiss.

When he pulled away from the kiss to look into her eyes, she brought his face down to hers for another kiss that made both of them dizzy. His hand slipped beneath her T-shirt to find her breasts and caress them tenderly. She moaned very softly and shifted her weight but didn't wiggle free of his embrace.

A few minutes later her T-shirt was off, and she wasn't sure how. Cassie threw it on the floor, then reached around her back and flipped the hooks until her bra was undone. She pitched it on the floor, too, and looked at Ted.

"Cassie...?" he questioned, reaching for her hand as she rose. "If you don't want to..."

"Shut the door, and lock it please," she said. "No, better yet, you lie still and I'll close the door."

"I love you," he murmured.

When she returned, she snuggled up next to him.

"Kiss me again, Ted. I love you too. I don't know what we're going to do about that later, but right now, it's enough."

———————

"That's Alicia and Daniel downstairs," Ted whispered. "We'd better—"

"We'd better get up and get dressed!" Cassie bolted upright. "Was that a mistake, Ted? Does it mean we can't get an annulment now?"

"Maybe, but we can always just get a divorce," he answered.

She struggled into her clothes and tossed his jeans and shirt at him. "Get dressed, lazy!"

Cassie had made him forget all about his still-weak arm and leg, but he was remembering them now.

The conversation between Alicia and Daniel stopped, and then they heard footsteps coming up the stairs. Cassie barely had time to open the bedroom door before Alicia made it to the top.

"Alicia, is that you?" Cassie yelled. "We're up here… cleaning."

Alicia stopped in the hallway and stared at the room as if she couldn't believe her eyes. "Ted, you are in John's room."

"I am," he said as he put his crutches under his arms and headed out of the room. "I thought it was about time, and Cassie has been helping me. You ready for the big night?"

"Yep, but I can't believe"—she swiped a tear from her eye—"that you have decided to do this. It's just the best graduation present you could give me."

"You don't think I'm stealing your thunder?" he asked.

"No! Of course not." She rushed over to hug him and almost toppled him over.

"It kind of seems like years have been dusted away, and I'm ready to remember John without so much pain," Ted said.

"Then there's no more ghosts to keep behind closed doors?" Alicia asked.

"Not a single one." Ted grinned.

"Thank you, Cassie." Alicia turned around and hugged her.

Cassie chuckled. "All I did was clean."

"No, you made my brother whole again," Alicia said. "Does Mama know?"

"Not yet, but I imagine she will when she sees the door open to this room," Ted told her as he started slowly making his way down the stair steps.

We're going to have an interesting life, Ted thought when he reached the bottom step. And he was finally ready to live it.

Chapter 11

TED SPENT MOST OF THE NEXT DAY ON A TRACTOR, FEELING truly healed even though his leg still twinged when he clambered up into the seat. But he didn't let it slow him down any.

He was grimy, sweaty, and whistling when he walked in the back door that evening. "What a wonderful day!" he announced to his father, Maria, and Cassie, who were still sitting at the supper table. "Summer is really here. I can feel it. My ankle feels better and my arm is getting stronger every day."

Clayton nodded. "I've been feeling livelier myself. Remember what Brock said, though. You don't want to get too frisky until those weak muscles in your leg heal."

When he said *frisky*, Ted saw Cassie bite back a smile.

"I'll try to remember that, Dad. I'm young and tough. I can handle a little friskiness."

Cassie turned bright red.

Clayton nodded again.

"Sit down, Son. We just finished supper, but your mother saved some food for you."

Maria brought a plate to the table. "I figured you'd be hungry. Working outside builds a hearty appetite. You haven't had much of one since you got hurt."

"Thanks, Mama. This looks pretty good. Is there more or did Cassie eat it all up from me?"

"Is this the man who's going to live in his great big cabin in the woods without a woman?" Cassie teased.

"Okay, okay!" Ted held up both hands in surrender. "I have to learn everything the hard way."

Her laughter reminded him of the fancy silver wind chimes his grandparents had sent his mother from south Texas.

Ted liked it when Cassie sat with him. She belonged there…permanently. Maybe not at that table but at another one on the property.

Maria stood up and started for the living room. "It's time for our movie night. You kids can join us when you get done if you want."

"Should we wait to start it?" Clayton pushed back his chair.

"No, but thank you," Ted answered. "Tell me something, Cassie," he said between bites. "If you could marry me all over again—if you decide that you want to, that is, after we divorce—what kind of wedding would you like?"

"Oh...I don't know," she said with a shrug. "I used to dream about an outdoor wedding, with my mama sitting in the front row of chairs. I wanted a white satin dress with a long veil and a longer train, and I wanted a big cake and a handsome groom to feed me most of it. But those were just my little girl dreams."

"And now that you are grown up?" Ted asked.

"Now I think what I want most is for someone to love me for just me. Not what they think I might be. Not for what they think they could make me into, but just me. I don't know what I want in a wedding, Ted. I don't care about all that foofaraw. But when I get married, I want a marriage, not just a wedding."

"Well, what do you care about?"

"Finding the right person to spend the rest of my life with. When I'm good and ready to settle down," she answered.

"Give me a hint. What kind of person would that be?"

"A kind and caring man who wants to love me for all eternity. That's all," she said with a slight smile.

"That's not the kind of man you want, Cassie." Ted

laughed, which annoyed her to no end. "You want someone to keep you on your toes, to keep you guessing about what's just around the corner of life, someone to hold and love you and hang in there and fight with you too."

"Oh, what would a pigheaded man like you know what a lady wants in a husband?" she snapped.

"Pigs aren't so bad once you get to know them." He laughed again. "They can be right friendly." This was the Cassie he liked best. The spitfire—not the one who sometimes seemed to think her life would turn out like a romance novel. All nice and neatly wrapped up by its happy ending, complete with a tame hero.

———

Cassie glared at him. He had agreed more or less not to talk about marriage, and he had somehow tricked her into doing just that. She wanted to smack him. She also wanted to throw her arms around his neck and kiss him until he melted like butter on hot biscuits. And she wanted to feel him kiss her back so that warm feeling he caused in her grew until it enveloped her whole body. She wanted to tell him a thousand times that she would *always* love him, but she couldn't. Yesterday had been beautiful, but in the long run, what if it was just putting the past to rest that had made them fall into bed together?

"Hmph," Cassie snorted. "Pigs don't know anything about love. I'm going to bed. I have to get up early. Enjoy your supper. It's stone cold by now and that serves you right."

Cassie left the kitchen and went straight up the stairs. Ted followed right behind her. When they reached her door, he pulled her roughly into his arms and against his broad chest. Then he tilted her chin back and kissed her lightly on the tip of her nose, her eyelids, and finally on her closed mouth.

"Oink, oink," he said when he let her go. He left her standing there, annoyed all over again, as he headed toward his own room.

Chapter 12

FINANCIAL RECORDS WERE ARRANGED IN NEAT STACKS ON the desk in front of Ted. He picked up one stack, rifled through it, shook his head, and set the papers back down. He wondered why he always waited until the last minute to do his personal taxes. Today was June 15, time for quarterly taxes. He had to have them in the mail by five o'clock, and he hadn't even begun.

Sunrays danced through the open window. He could almost hear the engine roar in his tractor or see the trout in the river swimming just under the surface of the water, waiting to be caught. Guy stuff—that's what he wanted to do. Not accountant stuff. Even a good fight with Cassie would be more fun than doing his taxes.

With a heartfelt sigh, Ted opened the computer program

to begin the report. On the payroll, he started to check the box marked *Single*, when he realized with a start that he could now file as a married man at the end of the year.

"Why didn't I think of that?" he wondered.

Uncle Sam didn't care how he had been married or why. He didn't care if Ted and Cassie had made love only one time or if they never had. They were legally married as far as the IRS was concerned.

Ted reached across his desk and dialed the clinic. Cassie usually answered the phone first, and she didn't disappoint him this time.

"Cassie?"

"Yes, Ted? Something wrong?"

"I don't think so," he said. "I'm working on my tax return, and it just dawned on me that I can file as married."

"Is being married a problem? Do I need to sign something?"

"No, but how about dinner at the Peach Orchard to celebrate me getting all this IRS stuff done? That will give me incentive to get it done and sent before you get off work," he said.

He heard a *click*, but he could still hear her voice.

"Good morning, ma'am. We'll be right with you. Please make yourself comfortable, and Gloria will call you as soon as Dr. Brock is ready for you," she said.

"Was that a yes or a no?" he asked when she was talking to him again.

"Yes, but can I come home and change before we go?" she asked.

"Of course." His heart was beating faster. "And if you don't take forever primping, we might drive up to Duncan and catch a movie after we eat. What would you like to see?"

"I don't care. So long as it's nothing with blood and guts. And I do not take forever to get ready to go somewhere," Cassie argued.

"Yes, you do. Sometimes I have to wait and wait for you," he argued right back. "That's not a good sign, you know."

"Oh, hush," she snapped. "You're not going to trick me into talking about marriage in that roundabout way. See you later when I finish up. I'll starve myself until tonight."

"Are we having a role reversal? Are you going to be the pig tonight?"

"I'm going to hang up on you right now."

Ted picked up his financial records and tax forms and started with a newfound sense of purpose. At noon Maria brought his lunch on a tray.

"Thanks, Mama. Sit down." He picked out a sandwich. "I've got a lot done so I can take a few minutes. You should've seen this desk an hour ago. It looked like a presidential aide from Washington, DC, dropped all the paper in the White House on it. I'm making progress, though."

His mother sat down in the leather chair in front of his desk. "Why are there so many papers for everything we do?"

"I just figured something out, Mama. Because of Cassie, I can file as married at the end of this year. That means I get a refund I wouldn't have gotten otherwise...about six thousand dollars more if I've got it figured right."

"Then buy Cassie a used car," Maria said. "If it weren't for her, you wouldn't have the money and you don't need it anyway. She shouldn't have to rely on us to take her everywhere she wants to go. I know there are days when I think she'd like to go shopping or just go for a drive, but she's not the kind to impose and ask."

"But—" Ted started.

"But what?" Maria said patiently. "Are you afraid if you buy her a car she will leave? Give her the freedom she needs. She knows who her heart belongs to and where home is but give her wings. If she loves you, she will come back to you. I've been thinking about that little house on the back forty that your great-grandparents built when they bought this land."

"I don't want her to leave." Ted stood up and paced. "I love her." He stopped and straightened up to his full height. "Are you suggesting what I think you are?"

"A woman likes to have her own kitchen and space, Son." Maria smiled. "That could be a nice little starter place for you until you can build something else. It's just two bedrooms and one bath, but it would be her place. I was young once, my dear, not too long ago. And I am a woman as well as a mother. I know a little about love." She got up and kissed him on the forehead and left, closing the door softly behind her.

In the middle of the afternoon his father wandered in carrying a tall glass of iced tea. "Thought you might be gettin' dry. Doing your taxes is hard work."

"Thanks for the tea. Yeah, this is about as exciting as watching the dust settle in the road when the cars go by," Ted said, glad for a little break. "Actually, I'm almost done. I just have to cross-check all the numbers and hit Send."

"Your mother tells me you'll get a big refund because you're married. She thinks you should buy Cassie a car. I agree with her," Clayton said.

"You're both right." Ted nodded. "But if I make it easy for her to leave... Well, what if she doesn't come back?"

"Betcha she does." His father's eyes twinkled. "Betcha

she's back here in six months. Let's make this interesting. You take her down to the little house and make her an offer, then give her the keys to a car. Not a new one. That would be flaunting your money. Get her something decent but used."

"How are we going to make it interesting?" Ted asked.

"I'll bet you one oil well—a producing one—against that ten acres of bottom land you bought last year. If Cassie doesn't come back in six months, you get the oil well. If she does come back, I get the land. If she never leaves at all, you get the oil well and you get to keep the land."

Ted grinned.

"Cassie would go up in flames if she thought we were betting on what she might or might not do."

"So would your mama. Keep it between us, Son." Clayton winked. "Better get going. You wouldn't want to keep Cassie waiting for her special evening out."

"How'd you know what I was planning?"

"I have my ways of finding things out," Clayton said as he headed for the door.

If everybody knew so much, why couldn't one smart little redhead know that he loved her? Ted thought crossly. And why did she *still* have to argue with him over every little thing? After the way they'd made love, the way she'd kissed him afterward, he wanted her to say that she was so happy she would never leave him.

He finished clearing off his desk, filed everything neatly, and was at the clinic by closing time to pick Cassie up.

―――――――

Cassie dashed upstairs to change. For the first time in weeks, her hair cooperated. It went up in a perfect French twist with springy little tendrils in front of her ears. She chose a pair of skinny jeans and a flowing white lace shirt, slipped her feet into a pair of sandals, and picked up her purse.

She waited in the living room for him to come down the stairs. "Well, now, who's waiting for whom? Here I am, starving to death, and you took forever to get ready. I'm so hungry, the next wind whistling through town could pick me up and blow me all the way to Arkansas."

"Sorry," he said. "You look absolutely beautiful, Cassie."

"You don't look so bad yourself." She smiled. "Are you trying to impress somebody?"

"Come on." He pulled her toward the door. "Before I throw you over my shoulder and have my way with you."

"Caveman." She giggled.

The drive from Ryan to Terral was only ten minutes, and

the parking lot of the café right next to the river bridge only had two cars in it. Ted helped her out of the car and ushered her into the Peach Orchard with his hand on her back.

His touch, as always, send her hormones into overdrive, and she wanted to stop and kiss him right there, but she kept walking. It wasn't a fancy place by any means, but the fish there was fabulous, and their pecan pie was to die for. Maybe not as good as what Maria made, but it came in a close second.

He chose a booth at the back of the dining area and sat down beside her instead of across from her. "You look better than anything on this menu."

"I should hope I look better than the catfish special," she said, laughing.

"What are y'all drinking, and are you ready to order?" the waitress asked. "Been a long time since I've seen you around, Ted. Is this your wife? I heard you got married a while back."

"I did, and this is Cassie," he answered. "Cassie, this is Avery Graham. I graduated with her from good old Ryan High School."

"Pleased to meet you," Avery said.

"Likewise." Cassie smiled at her. "And I'll have sweet tea and the full catfish dinner."

"Same here," Ted said. "But I want double fries with my order."

"Good to see you. I heard about your wreck. That must've scared Maria half to death," Avery said as she wrote on an order pad.

"She seems nice," Cassie said.

"She is." Ted nodded. "Our graduating class only had thirteen in it, so we were all pretty close. John went out with Avery a few times, but he never got serious about any girl."

"Did you?" Cassie asked.

"No, ma'am. I had a girlfriend or two, but then after John was killed, I didn't date much."

"And then you married me, right?"

"Best mistake I ever made." He grinned.

"So I'm a mistake?" she teased.

"Best one ever, and I'd do it all over again," Ted told her. "I've got good news. Because we're married, I will get a tax refund at the end of the year."

"That's nice." She didn't seem particularly interested.

"Cassie, hasn't it ever occurred to you that you could ask for half of everything I own when we get a divorce? We didn't even think about a prenup before we married so you are entitled to half of everything I own."

"Why would I do that?"

"You're doing it again." Ted shook his head. "You're asking a question instead of answering one."

"I don't want anything you have. Besides, what's half of what a dirt farmer has, anyway? Remember when I thought you were a dirt farmer?" She smiled. "Seriously, Ted, I don't want anything. You've been wonderful to me. You've changed my life. Your family is... I don't think I could find the words to say what they mean to me. I wouldn't do that to you, or them."

"I can't take anything from you, either, Cassie. I will get a refund because I deliberately overpay on my taxes. But because I am married now, I will most likely get back at least six thousand extra dollars. I—uh—want to buy you a car," Ted said and waited for her reaction.

"Nope," she said firmly. "You keep the money. I won't need a car. I can manage. You've done enough."

"I intend to buy you a car or a small pickup. You can't talk me out of it," he said.

"This looks good." Cassie picked up a piece of catfish. "And I said *no*. I don't want anything from you. Thanks all the same. It's sweet of you to think like that, but I want to do things on my own."

She looked at him in the candlelight, which cast soft shadows on his handsome face. She had assumed that his family had put him up to this. After all, the Wellmans didn't want for money. But how much had Ted made last year to get a refund for more than she and Deana had to live on for a whole year?

"Are you serious, or are you just spinning this tale so I'll let you buy me something?" Cassie asked.

"I'm as serious as a heart attack." He wasn't smiling. "Which is what I think you're trying to give me. That amount will buy an older car or truck, nothing new or fancy. If you want a new one, say the word and I'll get it for you."

"No," Cassie told him, "I don't even need a used one. But it would be nice not to have to be so dependent on everyone for rides."

"Then it's done." Ted picked up the ketchup bottle and squirted a layer on his fries.

"Just like that?" She snapped her fingers. "What if I get in it and drive away? I've been saving most of my money, and it's only a couple of months until I'm twenty-one. I could go somewhere and start all over. With the experience I've had at the clinic, I shouldn't have any trouble getting a job."

"I can't put a rope around you and make you stay in Ryan," he said.

You are a chicken if you don't apologize, her conscience singsonged. *You were dead wrong to attack him like that, and you know it.*

I won't, she argued with herself.

"I'm sorry." Cassie lost the argument. "Thank you for buying me a car. I was wrong to be hateful and I'm really sorry. Forgive me?"

"An apology from the Queen of Sass?" Ted's eyes twinkled a little.

"I said I was sorry. What do you want? For me to drop down on my knees and beg?" she said testily.

"That would be a sight to behold." Ted grinned. "Of course, I'd have to call the undertaker if you did because I've no doubt it would kill you to beg anyone for anything. Uncle Brock is going to buy Aunt Maggie a new car for her birthday. She's been driving the one she's got for about six years. I reckon I could get a good deal on it, or if you want to shop for something yourself, we can do that."

"Maggie's car would be fine." Cassie could hardly believe that in a couple of weeks she could have her own vehicle.

Chapter 13

CASSIE CAME DRAGGING HOME ON FRIDAY NIGHT THE NEXT week, so tired from a rushed day at the clinic that she just wanted a hot bath and a good romance book. She was almost too weary to even eat, but Liz and Justin had come home for the weekend to go to one of his cousins' weddings, and she couldn't be rude. So she changed into jeans and a shirt, tried to do something with her hair and finally pulled it up into a ponytail, and went to the supper table.

Liz had already set the table, and everyone had gathered around in the kitchen when Cassie arrived. Ted pulled a chair out for her and then sat down right beside her. The rest of the family, including Alicia's boyfriend, Daniel, found seats, and Clayton said a short grace. Then Maria began to pass food from one person to another.

"How was your day?" Ted asked Cassie.

"I'll answer for her," Brock said. "It was hectic, nerve-racking, and crazy. We were busy nonstop from the time we hit the clinic this morning until we finally got through the patient list and closed the doors. I couldn't have made it without Cassie."

Maria almost hummed with happiness as she passed a bowl of salad to Cassie. "This is an awesome day. My family is all around the table, and my mama is coming for a visit next week. Life is good."

"Yes, it is," Cassie agreed as she reflected on what her life might have been if Ted had not saved her from Cecil—twice now. She stole a glance over at him. He walked with only a very slight limp and his arm had healed. The few kisses, and that one time they'd had sex, replayed often in her mind.

Not sex, the pesky voice in her head scolded. *You two made love. Don't degrade what you had that day by calling it just sex.*

"Liz, how old were you when you and Justin got married?" Cassie needed to hear someone talk about themselves rather than listening to the annoying voice in her head.

"Eighteen." Liz smiled. "Justin turned twenty the day before we got married. He already had a year of college, and I was fresh out of high school. I had some concurrent college classes, so I had a semester, and I've been adding extra hours to my work load each semester. We're almost even now. We should be able to get into medical school at the same time, and when we finish that, we plan on doing a couple of years of Doctors without Borders before we start a family."

Cassie did the math in her head. Liz was twenty-one. She'd been married three years and had her life planned out for the next six or eight. Cassie would be her age in a few weeks, and she wanted to be a nurse more than anything, but her whole life wasn't planned.

But where do you want to live? This time it was Deana's voice.

With Ted, but is he in love with me only because I've helped him get over his past, or is it real? she answered.

"We must be almost the same age," Cassie finally said. "I'll be twenty-one in August."

Liz nodded. "I was twenty-one in March."

"And I won't be a grandmother for another decade," Maria moaned.

"You'll still be young," Alicia said, "but if you're in a hurry, Daniel and I…"

Maria held up a hand. "That's enough out of you. You and Daniel have college."

"But Mama, Liz was only eighteen when she got married," Alicia argued.

"I was more mature than you are," Liz teased.

"In your dreams, Sister!" Alicia protested.

Ted laid a hand on Cassie's shoulder and whispered, "Aren't you glad you're an only child?"

"No, I love this. I want more than one kid, but I also want to be a nurse," she answered.

Ted gave her shoulder a gentle squeeze and dropped his hand. "You can be both. You're smart and tough enough to be a mother and a nurse, you know."

Cassie's mother worked because she had to support a child, but she'd heard her mama say that if she had her way about things, she would be at home with Cassie every day. According to Deana, when a woman got married, she stayed at home and took care of things.

"But who will take care of the kids while I'm working?" she asked.

"Ever hear that old saying about how it takes a village to raise a child?" Ted grinned. "Well, look around you, Cassie. We've got a village."

A cold chill chased down Cassie's spine. She had only been with two boys before her mother died. They had been careful and remembered to use protection, but that night with Ted was a different matter. What if she was pregnant right then? She tried to figure out when her last period was, but she'd never been regular, and the stress of caring for Deana plus everything that had happened since then sure didn't make it any better.

She promised herself she would go to the drugstore the next day on her break and pick up one of those tests. Then she remembered how folks in small towns gossip and figured that wouldn't be a good idea. Maybe she could ask Ted to drive her to a Walmart store for some personal items and get one there. She'd have to hide it from him, but surely she could do that.

"How many kids do you want, Cassie?" Alicia asked.

"Maybe four," Cassie answered, but hoped that the first one wouldn't be arriving anytime soon.

"I want six," Alicia said.

Daniel groaned. "I guess I had better get two jobs, then."

"And we'll need a nanny with that many kids because I'm going to be a psychologist, darlin'," Alicia said.

"Four jobs." Daniel sighed. "I'll be a doctor in the day

and maybe a plumber in the evenings, then maybe work at being a bartender until the bars all close down."

"With Alicia's taste, you might want to think about not sleeping at all," Ted teased.

Alicia chunked her napkin across the table at her brother. Ted reached up and caught it in midair. "Mama, send her to her room."

"I've got a better idea." Alicia gave her brother a dirty look. "Why don't you make him go outside on the porch and not have dessert?"

"I'll take that." Ted pushed back his chair. "Cassie and I were going to take a walk anyway, so we'll just do it now."

Cassie had just finished her last bite, but she was looking forward to a slice of cherry pie with ice cream on top.

"I'll save both of you some pie," Maria whispered. "Go on with him and enjoy an evening walk."

Cassie nodded. "Yes, ma'am."

Ted laced his fingers with hers when they left the kitchen. "I should have asked you about this first. I'm surprised you didn't tell me to drop dead."

"I'm too tired to fight with you tonight," she told him.

"That's a good sign, because I've got something to show you," he said with a smile.

The sun was falling toward the western horizon, and fireflies flitted around them like little falling stars. The path that Ted led her down had been mowed recently, leaving behind the smell of fresh grass. Cassie remembered loving that scent when she and Deana mowed what little grass that they could sweet-talk into thriving in the backyard.

"Where are we going?" she asked.

"You'll see," Ted answered. "This used to be a road back before my grandparents built the big house. Now it's barely a path, but we might bring in some gravel and make a drive back here again."

"Why would you do that? Does it lead to an oil well?" Cassie was getting more curious by the minute.

"Just around this little bend, and then you'll see what's back here," Ted said.

"Oh! My!" She gasped when the house came into full view. Light flowed from all the windows. A wind had picked up and moved the porch swing back and forth, sending out a squeaking sound from the chains. She glanced over to the left to see a tire swing hanging from a huge pecan tree, and then over to the right to find Maggie's car parked not far from the freshly mowed yard. "How did Maggie get here? She didn't pass us on the path."

"This is the original Wellman home. My great-grandparents started here when this was all just farmland. Then they struck oil, but they didn't want to leave this little place. Years later my grandfather built the big house, and this one has sat empty for years. We've kept it maintained for sentimental reasons," Ted answered. "I've got the key. You want to go inside and see it?"

"I'd love to," Cassie said. "Is Maggie in there already? Is that why the lights are on?"

"So many questions." Ted chuckled as he unlocked the door. "Come on in and take a look around. Step right into the living room. Oak hardwood floors that my great-grandpa put down himself and that Granny Wellman kept shiny." It sounded like he was a real estate agent giving her the sales pitch. "Kitchen is straight ahead. Cabinets were built by Grandpa. Now back to the living room and down the hall to the two bedrooms, bathroom, and linen closet. For the time that it was built, the closets are large."

She stood in the middle of the oversized bathroom with a deep claw-foot tub on one side and a vanity on the other. "Two sinks were probably unheard of at that time too."

"Those were put in sometime down the line when the house was remodeled," Ted explained. "Here's the deal,

Cassie. My folks want to let us move into this place until I can build something better for you."

"Why would you want anything better?" Cassie asked. "This has history and love in every one of those hardwood planks on the floor."

"Is that a yes?" Ted asked.

"Can I think about it for a little bit?" She walked through every room again and imagined a big bed in the master bedroom, curtains on the window facing the east, and maybe a rocking chair over there in the corner. In the second bedroom, she could see a desk where she could study for her online courses, and maybe later, when she'd finished school, a baby bed over there by the window.

Ted walked up behind her and slipped his arms around her waist. "You know how I feel about you, Cassie. This will give us our own place to figure out if we want to stay married. Uncle Ash has talked to the judge, and of course the first question he asked was if our marriage had been consummated. I couldn't lie, so now we have to get a full-fledged divorce. It won't take any more time than an annulment and should be ready to sign on your twenty-first birthday. But we could live here and see how things go between now and then."

"I like that idea, but what about breakfast?" Cassie asked.

"I can cook, or you can," Ted whispered softly.

His warm breath on the tender spot of her neck sent shivers down her arms.

"Not that," she said and giggled. "I help Maria with breakfast every morning to pay for my room and board."

"Honey, we would be living here, so you wouldn't owe anything for that anymore," he said.

"Would we share a bed?" she asked.

"That's up to you," Ted answered. "I can bring in an extra bed and fix up one room for you."

"Can we go sit in the porch swing for a little while?" She needed time to think, and she dang sure couldn't do it with him so close that she caught a whiff of his shaving lotion every time she took a breath.

"Anything you want." Ted led her outside and pulled her down on the swing beside him.

She set the swing in motion with her foot, and then put her head on his shoulder. "This is like a mansion to me, Ted. I lived in a tiny trailer house with my mama until I was almost sixteen, and then my bedroom at Deana's had been a screened-in porch for years. They boarded it up, stuck a small window in one side and put a twin-size bed over against one wall. I would love to live here, but..."

Ted pulled a set of keys from his shirt pocket. "That car out there is yours. Maggie got her new one early and gave me a heck of a deal on that one. You can go and come whenever you want now, and if the time comes when you aren't happy, then I won't hold you back. My heart will be broken, but you've helped me learn to ask for help to get over that kind of thing. I want you to be happy with me, but if you can't, then I just want you to be happy."

"Are you serious?" Cassie thought she must be dreaming.

"Yes, ma'am. Will you please move in with me, Cassie?" Ted took her hand in his and kissed each of her knuckles.

"Yes, I will." She pulled his face down for a kiss. "When are we going to do this?"

"It will take a week for us to go through the barn where the excess furniture is stored. Mama never sells anything, so when she gets a hankering to redecorate, all the old stuff goes out in the barn. Mama Lita, that's my grandma, is coming up from Mexico next week, and we'll want to spend time with her, so at the end of next week?" Ted asked.

"That sounds good," Cassie answered. "Can I help pick out the furniture?"

"Of course." This time Ted kissed her.

She knew she'd made the right decision. It might not be right in a month or even two, but for now Ted had given her wings, not an anchor.

Chapter 14

Ted and his mother were sitting on the porch that Sunday afternoon when the big black car drove up the lane. "You expecting company?" Ted asked.

"Not until tomorrow when your Mama Lita arrives from Mexico," Maria answered.

"Someone must have made a wrong turn." Ted stepped out into the yard so he wouldn't have to yell, but a man got out of the car when it stopped, opened up the back door, and helped his grandmother and grandfather out of the vehicle. Then he went to the other side and helped Ted's great-grandmother out.

"Abuelita, we weren't expecting *you*!" Ted hugged his great-grandmother. "Mama Lita and Poppy, I'm so glad to see you. How did you ever talk Abuelita into coming with you?"

"We didn't." Poppy Rhodes shook his head. "She called your grandmother only yesterday and said that she wanted to come to Oklahoma with us. She also made it clear that she's not going home until you and Cassie are properly married in the church. She says it's not legal until the priest says it is. We may have to stay all summer."

Maria squealed like a little girl and ran out into the yard to hug her parents and grandmother. "What a wonderful surprise! We weren't expecting you until tomorrow, and we had no idea you were coming too, Abuelita."

"I have business to take care of. Ted has to be married properly. Is Cassie Catholic?" she asked.

"Yes, she is, but we can talk about all that later. Right now, we need to get you in the house and settled," Maria said. "Ted, honey, bring in their bags."

"I need a drink," Abuelita said. "Maybe a margarita. It's five o'clock in Mexico, and it's a hell of a long way from Oklahoma City all the way to this place."

"We can fix you right up with one," Maria told her. "Alicia, look who's here!" Maria yelled up the stairs.

"I am here to see to it my great-grandson is properly married, Maria. I'm glad Cassie is of our faith. She won't have to go to classes that way. We need to get busy planning the wedding."

Alicia ran down the stairs and folded Abuelita into her arms first, and then moved on to her Mama Lita and Poppy. "We didn't think you were coming until tomorrow."

"When my mama gets a burr in her britches, we have to go right then," Mama Lita said and laughed.

———————————

Cassie came out of the kitchen and hung back in the shadows a few minutes. The one they called Mama Lita was short like Alicia and had jet-black hair. Her dark-brown eyes were soft and friendly. The man they called Poppy wasn't much taller than his wife. Silver sprinkled his dark hair, and his eyes were so dark they looked black. It was the one they seemed shocked to see, Abuelita, which Cassie knew meant "little grandmother," that surprised her. The woman was even shorter than Alicia. She was dressed in a flowing dress with lots of embroidery that reached her ankles. Her gray hair was pulled back in a tight bun at the nape of her neck, and her green eyes twinkled when she looked at Ted.

"Cassie!" Ted spotted her. "Come and let me introduce you to my grandparents."

Cassie came out of the shadows and Abuelita took her

by the arms and looked her up and down for a full thirty seconds. "You have pretty red hair, but your hips look like you could bear children for my Ted after we get you properly married. Tomorrow, Maria will take me to see the priest, and we will set a time for a real wedding. I am tired. I have left my home and traveled in an airplane for the first time, so Ted, you and your fiancée can take my bags to my room. When I've had a drink, I will be ready for my nap."

"Maria, which room?" Cassie asked.

"The one beside Alicia's. The blue room. If I'd known you were coming, Abuelita, I would have had a room all fixed up." Maria looped her arm in Abuelita's and led her to the kitchen.

"I don't care where I sleep. I'm here to visit and to take care of things," Abuelita said.

"You got a beer?" Poppy asked. "Where's Clayton?"

"He went to put gas in the car so he could go and get you at the airport tomorrow," Maria said, "and beers are in the fridge. What would you like, Mama?"

"I would love an iced sweet tea," Mama Lita said.

"Ted, before you take the bags up to my blue room, come in here and talk to me," Abuelita called out. "We can have a drink together, and I can talk to your Cassie."

Ted dropped the bags he had in his hands, and Cassie did the same. "She's even bossier than my mother and my grandmother combined."

"I like her already," Cassie whispered. "But are we really going to have to go through with a church wedding?"

"Let's get her settled, and then we'll sneak off to our house and talk about that," Ted whispered as he draped an arm around Cassie's shoulders and ushered her into the kitchen.

"I know how you met and let the justice of the peace marry you, but I want to hear how you fell in love with each other." Mama Lita patted the chair beside her.

Maria quickly made a snack tray with cheese, crackers, and fresh fruit while Alicia made a blender of margaritas. "Let's talk first about your trip."

"It was fine," Mama Lita said and then turned to Cassie, who had sat down beside her. "When did you fall in love with my Ted?"

"And Ted, when did you fall in love with Cassie?" Abuelita reached for a strawberry when Maria put the tray on the table.

"How do you know we're in love?" Ted asked.

"By your eyes and the way you look at each other," Mama Lita said. "I can see this is embarrassing both of you, so we'll talk about that later. Go ahead and take our bags up to our rooms, Ted."

"Cassie, you can stay right here with me," Abuelita said.

"Yes, ma'am," Cassie said, smiling.

"It has always been my hope to see my grandchildren married and settled before I die. Now all we have to do is get Alicia down the aisle and I can die in peace." Abuelita sighed.

"Daniel and I are going to live together for four years and then get married, and you are not going to die, Abuelita. You have to live to see your great-great-grandbabies." Alicia brought out a margarita glass and set it, along with the pitcher, in front of her great-grandmother. "We are going to elope to Las Vegas when we get married. No fuss, no muss."

"You"—Abuelita shook her finger at Alicia—"will marry in the church like a good girl should, and you will not live with Daniel until you are blessed by the priest. I will put you in a convent if you do."

"I'm just teasing you," Alicia said.

"I'm not teasing." Abuelita frowned. "My Maria did not raise a girl to shack up with a boy."

Cassie felt the heat rising to her cheeks. She and Ted were legally married, but they were about to "shack up" to see if it would work, and this little woman wasn't going to make her get married again, not in a church or anywhere else.

———————

Late that night, in the wee hours of the morning, Ted laced his hands behind his neck and sighed again, for the hundredth time. He'd made Cassie happy—truly happy—and that made him feel remarkably good. He was thinking about the way she'd kissed him for his simple gift when he heard a faint knock on the door.

"Come in," he said softly, not really so very surprised to see her sneak in the door and cross the room to his bed.

"Ted, I can't sleep," she whispered.

"I can't either."

He rolled over in his bed and propped himself up on one elbow. Even in the dim glow from the hall light, Cassie could see that he was bare-chested. The covers were drawn up only to his waist.

"Come here, Cassie."

The look in his dark eyes dared her to say no.

She didn't.

Cassie locked the door with a faint but definite *click*. She raised her nightshirt over her head, revealing nothing but milky skin underneath.

She was as beautiful as any goddess in her nakedness, and he pulled her under the covers with him and ran his hands over her body. Her mouth sought his, demanding kisses... and more.

"God Almighty," he gasped. "Cassie, you are so beautiful. I love you so much. Don't ever leave me. I'd do anything to keep you..."

"Shh." She put her fingers over his mouth. "We don't need to talk about that now. Make love to me, Ted. The way you did the first time. I want you—*now*."

Ted held her close afterward for the longest time, until she opened her eyes and smiled up at him.

"Oh, Ted. That was...wonderful."

"Mmmm," he agreed sleepily.

"Would you mind...if we start all over again?" she whispered.

"Why, Cassie...that's exactly what I had in mind," he whispered back.

Chapter 15

CASSIE PACED THE LIVING ROOM FLOOR RESTLESSLY. SHE picked up a magazine and tossed it aside. She tried to read her latest romance novel, but she couldn't keep her mind on it. Evidently, she was in one of her Jesus moods, as her granny used to call them. Granny had said that Cassie didn't know what she wanted, wouldn't want it if she got it, and Jesus himself couldn't live with her.

Finally, she went out to sit on the porch and breathe in the fragrance of the roses. Maybe she would work this restlessness out of her mind while the frogs chirped and the locusts did their nightly singing. But the night was too hot for frogs, and the locusts were silent that night.

Ted came around the house. "Hi."

"Supper's over already. Maria has taken your

grandmothers to Duncan to buy groceries, but she left you a plate in the oven."

His boots were caked with mud and his once-white T-shirt looked like it had been fished up from the bottom of the Red River. The dust in his hair made it look brown instead of black, and a fine rim of dirt lined his forehead where his hat had been.

"I'm hungry as a bear. Let me shuck these dirty clothes and take a shower. Maybe I'll bring my plate out here and eat on the front porch." He disappeared before Cassie could tell him that nobody, and she meant nobody who still needed air to breathe, wanted to be in the same county with her when she was in a mood like this.

She finally sorted through her feelings long enough to realize that this mood had settled because she hadn't been up-front and honest with Abuelita. She liked the woman, but that old gal wasn't going to tell her what or what not to do.

Ted backed out of the door, carrying his supper on a tray. He sat down beside Cassie.

"I'd like to show you something when I finish eating," he said. "Okay with you?"

She started to snap at him and tell him she didn't want to

see anything. What she wanted to do was run away and never look back.

"Not very talkative tonight, are you?" Ted popped a chunk of buttered biscuit into his mouth.

Cassie shook her head.

"What's on your mind?"

"You don't want to know," she answered.

"Hey, if you want to be alone, just say so. I know how you feel. There's been times when I damn sure didn't want to be talked to. After John died there were times I thought I would scream when people talked to me."

"I think I would like to be alone," she said.

He picked up his tray and kissed her lightly on the forehead. "I still want to show you something later if you want. If not, you can see it another time. Come and get me if you want company." Ted crossed the porch and went back into the house.

He finished his supper in the kitchen, quietly climbed the stairs to his bedroom, flopped down on the bed, and tried to make some sense of Cassie's mood. He hoped that she wasn't thinking of getting into her car and leaving.

There was a gentle knock on his door.

"Yes?" he answered.

Cassie opened the door. "Can I come in?"

"Sure."

"I'd like to see what it is you wanted to show me, but if you're tired…"

"Come sit beside me." Ted patted the edge of the bed.

She left the door open and sat on the edge of the bed. He took her small hand in his big one. "Are you in a better mood?"

She smiled. "Yep."

"What's so funny?"

"I get in these moods sometimes," she said. "Granny called them my Jesus moods. I'm pretty hard to live with when I'm in the middle of one. She said I didn't know what I wanted, and wouldn't want it if I got it, and Jesus himself couldn't live with me then."

"I'll try to remember that in the future." He gave her hand a warm squeeze. "I guess I don't stand a chance if the man from Galilee couldn't live with you."

"What did you want to show me? The inside of your bedroom? I've seen it," she teased.

Ted grabbed her and pulled her down beside him and covered her face with kisses.

She didn't push him away, but just enjoyed the way his

lips on her eyelids, the tip of her nose, her neck, and most of all her lips made her feel.

"No, I don't want to show you my bedroom." He rolled off the other side of the bed and picked up his sneakers. "Would you please go put on some shoes? We're going to take a walk, and it could be past midnight when we get back." Ted hopped off the bed, tugged his shoes on and then a T-shirt.

"Okay," she agreed. "I'll be downstairs in five minutes. Betcha I beat you."

They met at the top of the stairs in two minutes, both out of breath and giggling.

"Be back later," Ted yelled over his shoulder at Alicia and Daniel as he and Cassie left by the back door.

Once they were in the yard, Ted took Cassie's hand and paced his steps to hers. "We're going back to the house we're going to live in real soon."

They walked in silence for a while, breathing in the hot night air and listening to the crickets' serenade.

"You said we could move in this weekend, but Abuelita has different ideas," Cassie said.

He pulled her closer to him, dropped her hand and draped an arm around her shoulders. "The law says we're married. Someday, when you are ready, we might have a simple ceremony at the church, but that's all up to you. And we are moving into our house this weekend."

"Thank you for that," Cassie said. "It takes a load off my mind. Now what are you going to show me about the house?"

"I promised you that you could help pick out the furniture and all the stuff, and we can change it all out, so if there's anything you don't like, we can go back to the barn. And here is my surprise." He led her up onto the porch and opened the door. "Not even Mama or Alicia have been in here."

"Oh, Ted, it's beautiful," she said. "I love the soft colors and the sheer drapes that let the light in, and even those throw pillows. You should be a decorator."

His grin told her volumes. "Want to see the rest?"

She squealed at the four-poster bed in the master bedroom, but when she saw the empty room across the hall, she raised an eyebrow. "Why didn't you put something in here?"

"Because you should design your office, not me," Ted answered.

She threw her arms around his neck and kissed him— long, lingering, and passionate.

When the kiss ended, he dropped down on one knee and pulled a red velvet box from his pocket. "Cassie Wellman, you make me happy, and angry, and you've brought me back to life. Will you marry me?"

She held out her left hand. "Ted Wellman, we are already married," she said.

"That wasn't real. This is." Ted popped the box open.

Her eyes grew wider and wider, and then tears flowed down her cheeks. "How did... When..." she stammered.

"Whenever you say the word. I'm not rushing you, but I want us to be engaged," he said.

"Those are my grandmother's rings," she whispered, "the ones I sold for money to leave Texas."

"Yes, they are. I called every pawn shop in Sweetwater until I found them and bought them back. If you'd rather have another set..." he asked, still on his knees.

"Yes, I will marry you," she said. "Let's just do a simple wedding at the church this weekend. But first, did you really mean it when you said I was smart and tough enough to raise a family, go to school, and work all at the same time?"

"I did." He slipped the ring on her finger, and she dropped down on her knees in front of him. "I meant every word of it, darlin'."

"Well, I'm glad because I'm pregnant," she told him.

Ted gathered her up into his arms and held her tightly

against his chest, both of their hearts doing double time in unison. "Oh, darlin', you've just made me the happiest man on this earth."

"For real?" she muttered. "You're not upset with me? I didn't even think of protection that night we..."

"Upset?" Ted chuckled. "We're starting a family. Can we name him John if he's a boy?"

"Of course," Cassie said, "but let's not tell anyone until after we've said our vows in the church."

Chapter 16

THE WEDDING WAS PLANNED FOR SEVEN O'CLOCK AT THE church with only family in attendance. Maria and the grand-mothers had been busy all day making a Mexican wedding cake and food for the reception. They had invited dozens of people to come by, and the living room was already filled with gifts.

Cassie woke at five that morning after a restless night. She kicked off the covers and opened the drapes. The leafy trees rustled in the warm breeze, displaying several shades of green.

"Cassie!" Alicia burst into the room without knocking. "Today is the day and I'm so nervous I'm about to puke! What if I stumble going down the aisle? What if my hair won't fit in the circlet of rosebuds you chose? I want everything to be perfect for you and my brother's wedding, even if it is a small affair."

"You're giving me a case of nerves." Cassie hoped that she didn't develop morning sickness on her wedding day, or on the honeymoon either, for that matter.

"You'll do fine," Alicia said. "You're the strongest woman I've ever met, and this whole family is so lucky to have you. Let's go grab a sweet roll and get some milk to calm both of our jittery stomachs. What I really need is a good stiff shot of tequila. Liz is already up and says to just call her when we're ready for her to do our nails and put our hair in rollers. She swears those little pink sponge rollers hold the curls longer than a curling iron." Alicia rambled on and on.

Somehow the day passed. Liz had given both girls a mani-pedi and then fixed their hair, and it was time to put Cassie in her dress.

"I want to thank you again, Liz"—Cassie gazed at the beautiful white dress hanging on the back of the door—"for letting me borrow your dress."

"I hope it brings you as much luck in marriage as it has me." Liz grinned. "Maybe someday later, when our little sister grows up, we'll have it altered for her."

"Oh, no!" Alicia shook her head. "I don't want a straight dress like that. I want yards and yards of satin and lace."

"Have you seen Ted? Is he okay? All of this isn't going to make him revert back to..." Cassie paused.

"Ted is fine," Alicia said. "He just wishes y'all would have had a morning wedding, but he is happy that you agreed to a weeklong honeymoon."

"I can't seem to refuse him anything." Cassie smiled.

"That's a good thing," Abuelita said as she came in carrying a cup of coffee. "You are doing this right. No great-granddaughter of mine is going to elope. This is the best day of your life, a day you will always remember."

"Abuelita, what if Ted decides to fall out of love with me?" Cassie asked as she put on her dress. "How did you know you were doing the right thing when you married?"

Abuelita set the cup down on the end table and patted Cassie on the arm. "Why do you young women doubt your hearts? You worry your mind about matters your heart would not question. Ted loves you. Make today the most important day of your life, and tomorrow will take care of itself."

"I love you." Cassie kissed her on the cheek.

Abuelita smiled. "You and Ted are good together. You are

very smart and very strong. God did good when he put you together."

"Is this really me?" Cassie asked when she looked at her reflection in the mirror. "Liz, my hair is gorgeous and this dress fits like it was made especially for me."

"It was," Liz said. "We just didn't know it at the time."

"You are beautiful." Alicia sighed. "In four years, Daniel and I will get married. Don't tattle on us, but we are going to live together while we go to school. Mama knows, but we're not telling the grandmothers."

There was a soft knock on the door and Clayton pushed it open. "I hear there's a bride in here that needs a ride to the church."

Cassie smiled. "That would be me, and my two brides-maids here are going in the truck with me."

"Ted is already at the church. Want to know what he asked me today? He wanted to know how he would ever live if you changed your mind at the last minute."

"Never happen," Cassie said.

Ted waited at the front of the church with Father Patrick, his dad, and Justin, who were serving as his groomsmen. He'd been nervous all day, but when the music started playing, signaling that the bride was about to enter the church, his hands grew clammy. Then Alicia and Liz took forever, probably just to torture him, coming down the aisle.

When Cassie stepped into the door with her arm looped in Poppy's, all of Ted's nerves settled. She really was going to marry him. She wasn't going to get in her car and run away, leaving him behind with a broken heart.

"Who gives this woman to be married to this man?" the priest asked finally.

"This whole family accepts her into our family and gladly gives our blessing for this marriage," Poppy said and then sat down in the front row beside Mama Lita.

Ted said his vows, participated in the full mass, and somehow got through the whole ceremony. When the priest said that he could kiss the bride, Ted swore he felt a brush of cold wind across his face.

I'm free now. John's voice popped into his head. *I'm happy for you, Brother.*

———————————————

When they were back at the house, the newlyweds led the first dance out on the massive front lawn where the reception was held. Twinkling lights lit up the trees, and a full dinner was spread out on several buffet tables.

After the reception was over, Cassie Stewart O'Malley Wellman took off her gorgeous mint-green sundress, put on a pair of jeans, and ran out of the house in a rainstorm of birdseed. She stopped long enough to throw the bouquet that Ted had bought the day they got married in Texas over her shoulder, straight into Alicia's hands.

"Get ready, Mama, to plan another one!" Alicia held the bouquet over her head and did a happy dance.

It was almost midnight when the small private plane landed in Mexico City and a car took them to a condo right on the beach. Cassie peeled out of her jeans and T-shirt and shook her hair free, letting it fall in natural ringlets to her shoulders.

"I love you," Ted said as he drew her into his arms and out to the beach.

"Ted, I'm only wearing my underwear," she said.

"And we have the only beach house for five miles up and down this beach. Abuelita owns this whole area, and no one can see us. I want to see you in the moonlight," he said.

"I love you," she said.

"I love you, too, and I'm not sure a week is enough of a honeymoon," Ted said.

"Shhh." She touched his lips with her fingertips. "We'll live one moment at a time. Fate gave us an unusual start, but darlin', we will make the most of our fifty or sixty or maybe seventy years together. After all, we are still young, so we're going to do what an old country music song says and love each other for a long, long time."

"I'm not going to argue." Ted scooped her up and took her back inside the beach house.

"Neither am I," she whispered.

Love sultry, small-town romance?
You're in for a real treat! Read on for a look at

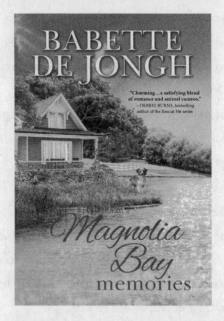

in the Welcome to Magnolia Bay
series from Babette de Jongh.

Chapter 1

ADRIAN CRAWFORD PARKED HIS LEXUS LC 500 CONVERTIBLE at the loneliest corner of the new animal shelter's gravel lot. Far from the handful of other vehicles and even farther from the centuries-old oaks that draped their scaly, fern-covered branches over the chain-link fence, the birthday bonus he'd given himself last month would be safe.

The construction/renovation of the shelter had progressed significantly since his last visit a week ago. The old Craftsman-style home's exterior face-lift was complete. Quinn, Adrian's old college buddy and the contractor in charge of the project, had already put up the new sign by the entrance. The sign, handmade with white lettering on a bluebird-blue background, matched the new paint and trim on the old house.

A bit bright for his taste, but as a business consultant

working pro bono for the nonprofit shelter, it wasn't his place to argue with the three women in charge of this project. And Quinn was so crazy in love with the trio's leader, Abby, that he wasn't thinking straight.

"*Furever Love*," Adrian scoffed. "What kind of name is that for a business?" The unfortunately cutesy name the women had chosen for the shelter arched across the top of the sign in a curlicue font they had agonized over for hours. Beneath that, in more sedate lettering: Magnolia Bay Animal Shelter.

Adrian pushed the button to close the car's top. He left the windows open a few inches to keep the car's interior from baking in the Louisiana summer sun. Halfway to the shelter's front porch, he pointed the key fob behind him and pressed the button to lock the car with a quiet but satisfying *blip-blip*.

"Gang's all here." Quinn's truck was parked by the outdoor dog runs, where the sound of heavy machinery droned. Reva—the organizing force behind the shelter even though her niece, Abby, was officially in charge—lived at the farm next door. Abby and Quinn were living on-site in the old estate's pool house until the shelter's grand opening, so unless Quinn was making a hardware store run, they were always here.

"Well, almost everyone's here." Heather's car, he noticed, was conspicuously absent.

Typical. Heather was just about always late. Adrian couldn't help but wonder why Abby and Reva thought they could trust her to be in charge of the day-to-day operations when she couldn't even make it to their weekly meetings on time.

Reva's dog, Georgia, trotted across the parking lot, coming toward him with a proprietary air. She was a funny-looking combo of dog breeds: a short, long dog with a thick speckled coat of many colors and a white-tipped tail that curved over her back. Her brown eyespots drew together in a concerned frown as she sniffed his jeans and then the treads of his new Lowa hiking boots. When she completed her inspection, she looked up at him with a "state your business and I'll decide if you can come in" attitude.

He knelt to pet Georgia's head. "I'm here to brainstorm with the team about another grant proposal for funding, if you must know."

Then he scoffed at himself. Quinn, Abby, Reva, and Heather all talked to animals like they were human. Now he was doing it too. "Assimilation is nearly complete," he told Georgia in his best imitation of the Borg.

Georgia stiffened and growled at something behind Adrian. He turned and looked, then bolted to his feet. The scruffy old black-and-white tomcat who'd been hanging around the area was walking tightrope-style along the top of the chain-link fence near Adrian's car. "Don't you do it..."

He could tell by the direction of the cat's gaze that he was about to jump from the fence to the hood of Adrian's brand-new, never-been-scratched car. "No!" He started running, but the cat was already gathering itself for the leap. "Bad cat!"

Too late.

Georgia took off like an avenging army of one, galvanized into action and ready to tell the cat what for, announcing her intention with a high-pitched, yodeling bark.

The cat was already mid-leap with front paws extended, body stretched out, and back toes spread when he spotted the dog barreling toward him. Eyes wide, mouth frozen in a grimace of terror, the cat twisted in midair to go back the way he'd come. Too late.

His spine hit the hood of Adrian's car with a loud *thwump*, then his body twirled like a corkscrew, all claws extended as he scrambled to get his balance.

"No..." Adrian ran, but Georgia ran faster. She leaped up, scrabbling at the side of the car in an impossible effort to reach the cat. Never gonna happen; Georgia wasn't even knee-high. But she didn't know it, the cat didn't know it, and none of that mattered to the previously shiny, immaculate finish of Adrian's new car.

"No, shoo, bad dog," Adrian yelled. Why hadn't he used the perfectly good, fitted canvas cover that he'd left in the trunk of the car? "Get down, right now." Why hadn't he bothered to toss it over the car the second he got out? "Hush, dog." He tried to push the dog away with his foot. "Get back. Go home."

The cat leaped up to the car's convertible top and hissed down at the dog, who barked even more ferociously, moving to scratch a different area on the side of Adrian's poor car. He snatched the little troublemaker up.

The little dog whined and squirmed but didn't bark. The cat, frozen in a bowed-up caricature of a Halloween cat, stopped growling long enough to catch his breath. In the sudden cessation of noise, Adrian heard a sound behind him.

Reva rushed up, all flowing hair and patchwork fabric—a prematurely gray hippie. She snatched Georgia out of his arms. "I'll put her up," she said. "You grab the cat and bring him inside. We've been trying to catch him for weeks."

As Reva hurried back across the parking lot with her

Birkenstocks scuffing along the gravel surface, Adrian stood with his hands on his hips, surveying the damage. These scratches were not the sort that could just be buffed out with a good coat of Minwax. "Son of a bitch."

But there was nothing he could do about the damage now. He heaved a sigh and plowed his hands through his hair, then applied his business-consultant problem-solving skills to the situation. "Okay." First things first. "Come here, cat."

He held his hands out to the cat and made kissy noises. The cat backed away, growling low in his throat. "Naw, don't be that way." Adrian softened his tone even further. "Come on, little man." The cat *was* little but also a fully grown tomcat with a big jughead jaw. "Here, kitty, kitty."

The cat glared at him, so he used one of the tricks he'd heard Reva mention when she was talking to the shelter girls about taming wild cats. He half-closed his eyes, looking sleepily at the cat and blinking slowly. The cat settled onto his haunches, his glowing amber eyes not as wide-open as before.

Well, fuck me, he thought. It worked.

He started humming, not a tune, just random low tones.

The damn cat started purring, and damn if he didn't start doing that slow blinking thing too.

Which Adrian realized he had forgotten to keep doing, so he started it up again. His humming resembled a tune he'd heard his grandmother sing, so he added words to the tune: "What's up, stinky cat?" The cat did stink. He smelled like dirt, motor oil, and cat pee. "Whoa, whoa, whoa... Come here, stinky cat; whoa, whoa, whoa..."

The cat's body tensed, raising up a fraction off his haunches as if preparing to run.

Yeah, that shit wasn't working, so he went back to humming. The cat settled back down. He didn't seem inclined to move toward Adrian's outstretched hands, but at least he wasn't running or hissing or growling. Adrian eased forward and gently touched the cat, spreading his fingers lightly over the cat's bony ribs.

The cat's purring stopped. Adrian kept his fingertips on the cat's haunches, letting the skittish feline get used to him before he pushed the envelope any further. He did more of the blinking thing, still humming, and slowly began to stroke the cat's scruffy, greasy, black-and-white fur. It seemed peppered with tiny scabs.

No question, this dude was a fighter.

Adrian eased his fingers farther along the cat's back, then slowly dragged him forward. The cat resisted at first, but at some point in the process, he padded along the car's hood toward Adrian, assisted by the gentle pressure Adrian kept applying. They seemed to have reached some sort of unspoken agreement. Making soothing sounds, not even a hum anymore but a vibration in his throat that he could feel but barely hear, Adrian gathered the reluctant cat into his arms.

———————

Cat let the man hold him close, only because the hands that held him didn't grab too tightly or try to force anything. Cat knew, somehow, that if he changed his mind about accepting help, the man would let him go.

Cat had never been given any other name, though he had been called many different versions of it. As he rode along in the man's arms—carried toward the building into which he'd seen other cats come and go of their own free will—Cat thought of the many names he'd been called.

Damn Cat. Fucking Cat. Asshole Cat. Go Away Cat.

His personal favorite up until now: Go Away You Damn Fucking Asshole Cat.

That one had always seemed particularly impressive to him.

But this man called him by a new name, one that Cat

much preferred because of the tone in which it had been uttered. Stinky Cat. He liked that one. He decided that would be the name by which he would refer to himself, whenever he wanted to think of himself as a cat with a name.

Despite the man's gentle reassurance, Stinky Cat felt himself becoming increasingly tense as they neared the door that would soon close behind him, cutting off the option of changing his mind.

He wanted to believe. He wanted to be like those other cats who seemed so confident, so unafraid. They even sat with the dogs—napped with them on the building's wide front porch!—and everyone seemed perfectly content. Even the bad little dog who'd come after him was nice to those other cats. She licked their ears the way mama cats licked their babies.

But Stinky Cat had a bad feeling that the dog he'd heard called Georgia wasn't going to lick his ears. She might not have used her teeth on him as she'd threatened to do, but she made it clear she didn't want him around. She had been ready to chase him right back over the fence he had climbed. He had wanted to see more of this strange place in which dogs and cats and people seemed to get along much better than the dogs and cats and people of his previous experience, who were more inclined to try to kill one another.

But now he wasn't so sure he was up for the challenge. He pushed his front paws against the man's supporting arm and leaned his head back against the man's chest.

"Shhh," the man said, "You're okay." Then he stopped walking and stood still, halfway between the metal hill Cat had been stranded on and the building where the dogs and cats came and went whenever they pleased. "Nobody's going to hurt you."

Stinky Cat didn't know what the words meant, and he was too worried about what might happen to understand the man's thoughts. But the tones of the man's voice soothed him, just as the man's fingers stroking his fur soothed him. He felt himself purring again, relaxing against the man's comforting bulk almost against his better judgment. He knew this human wouldn't harm him intentionally, as so many others had.

But he wasn't sure about the people inside that building.

Stinky Cat wanted to see if he could be one of those cats who seemed so confident and happy and unafraid. But he worried that something terrible may have happened to the ones who were caught in the traps. That's why he'd been so careful to avoid the wire tunnels that held enough fish-scented food to fill his belly for days. He'd been too afraid to risk it.

He'd been afraid all his life—or at least from the moment

in early kittenhood when he'd woken with his siblings to find that their mother was gone. He even slept afraid—and lightly enough to wake completely between one breath and another, his ever-present fear fueling his ability to escape or fight for his life if a predator pounced.

Fear had kept him alive this long.

How could he give it up now?

Adrian had the damn stinky cat within ten feet of the shelter's front porch when he heard Heather's car coming. He knew it was hers because of the loud rattling sound the old Honda's hinky motor made. She always brought her kids and her badly behaved dog. Knowing there was a high probability of mayhem about to ensue, he petted the cat and took another few, slow steps, hoping to make it inside the building before the car skidded into the parking lot. "What's up, stinky cat," he sang. "Whoa, whoa, whoaah."

Tamping down the sense of urgency that kept creeping into his head and infusing his tone, he took a few cautious steps closer to the shelter. Balancing the need to move in sync with the cat's fluctuating degree of compliance with the imperative of getting inside before...

Heather's car careened into the parking lot, scattering gravel. The dog's head hung out the window, barking as if he had something important to say.

The cat's claws came out like Wolverine's knives. Intent on escaping, the frightened feline dug those claws into Adrian's flesh, slicing effortlessly through his shirt. The back claws gained traction by digging deep into Adrian's abs, while the front claws latched onto his chest. The determined cat used his claws like grappling hooks to haul himself up to an unsteady perch on Adrian's shoulder, where with one last, mighty effort, he launched off Adrian's back and hit the ground running.

Before Adrian could gather the presence of mind to say, "Ow, shit," the cat had scaled the chain-link fence and leaped into the thick underbrush on the other side.

Adrian watched Heather park her rattletrap car under the shade of a live oak whose trailing, fern-covered branches were as thick as a full-grown human body. She clearly had more trust in the universe—or her car insurance—than he did.

Heather's dog—a honey-and-brown speckled Aussie with flashy copper-and-white markings—rushed up to greet him. Adrian reached down to pet the dog's head. "Hello, Jasper. You don't even realize that you just ruined everything, do you?"

Jasper panted with enthusiasm, wagged his whole back end, and grinned a doggy grin.

A second later, Heather's son, Josh, ran up to bombard Adrian with the latest news. "I got in trouble at school today. See?" He pointed to a small bruise on his cheekbone. His wheat-blond hair stuck up in clumps, and his navy-blue polo shirt was gray from what must have been a sweaty altercation on the school playground.

"Wow, I bet that hurt." Adrian gave what he hoped was sufficient attention to the almost nonexistent but clearly exciting wound. "Did the teacher punch you?"

"No, silly." Josh grinned, revealing a gap where he'd recently lost a tooth. "Teachers don't get to punch kids."

"What happened, then?"

"I pushed Kevin for calling me a crybaby, and then he punched me. We both got in trouble, and Ms. Mullins— she's the principal now—said we'll have to apologize to each other in the morning, but after that, we're gonna forget all about it."

"Uh-huh."

"As long as it doesn't happen again," Heather added with a stern look at Josh. She and Josh's twin sister, Caroline, walked toward them hand in hand. Caroline seemed to be the complete opposite of her brother. Wearing a still-pressed-looking jumper, her white blouse and socks neat and clean, her long blond braids tied with crisp blue ribbons, Caroline was as reserved as Josh was outgoing.

Adrian couldn't help noticing how cute Heather looked, even dressed as she was in slightly baggy jeans and a simple white blouse with a modest neckline. What seemed like a deliberate effort to hide her femininity wasn't working. Had never worked, in fact, at least as far as he was concerned.

The needy kid who now clung to Adrian's leg in an effort to regain his attention kept him from reaching out to touch the bright blond curl that had escaped Heather's haphazard ponytail. It wasn't that the kid was physically in the way because if Adrian wanted to touch Heather, no one would be able to stop him. What stopped him was the fact that she had kids.

It wasn't because Josh's attention-seeking behavior could be exhausting.

It wasn't because Caroline was so unbearably shy that she often hid behind Heather with her thumb in her mouth.

It wasn't because Erin, the willowy girl who strolled toward the shelter with her nose in her phone, was prone to flare-ups of teenage angst.

There wasn't anything wrong with Heather's kids in particular. If not for all the hangers-on in her life, Adrian would have been up for a quick fling with her, as long as it came with a flexible expiration date. But her kids were a major part of her deal—as they should be—and he wasn't emotionally ready to be a stepdad.

So he kept his distance, and she kept hers.

She surprised him by reaching out and touching his chest. Her fingers spread across the fabric of his T-shirt, lightly stroking, barely even a touch at all. "You're bleeding."

Had she not seen what just happened? "That's the usual result of being climbed like a tree by a freaked-out cat."

"Oh?"

"Yeah, Mom," Josh supplied. "Adrian was holding that black-and-white cat y'all have been trying to catch."

Her eyebrows went up, two delicate blond arches of surprise over her wide, leaf-green eyes. "You caught him?"

"I *had* caught him, yes. I was almost at the shelter with him in my arms when y'all drove up."

"Jasper barked, and the cat went nuts." Josh hopped with excitement at the remembered event. "Huh, Adrian?"

He smiled down at the kid. "That sums it up."

Heather's pretty face was windowpane easy to read. Her

cheeks washed with pink, and she brought a hand up to cover her mouth. "I'm so sorry!"

"Jasper tried to chase it when we got out of the car." Josh tugged on Adrian's shirt, encouraging him to look down. "But it ran too fast, didn't it, Adrian? It was already over the fence by then."

Adrian looked down and put his hand on the kid's shoulder. "Yep, it was."

"Lord help us," Heather said softly, her voice breathless, which had an unsettling effect on Adrian's peace of mind. "I am so sorry Jasper caused all this trouble."

As if to underscore her comment about Jasper, the dog took off after another of Reva's cats from next door who was stalking something in the shrubbery by the shelter's front porch.

"Jasper," Heather yelled. "Get back here."

The overexcited dog paid zero attention.

"Josh, Caroline, please go get that dog and put him in one of the kennels out back."

Josh ran after the dog and grabbed him by the collar. Caroline followed more slowly. "Caroline," Heather called out. "Open and close the gates for Josh, okay?"

Caroline changed course, heading for the walk-through gate that led to the kennels. "Yes, ma'am."

"Make sure they are securely latched once you go through, okay?" Even though there weren't yet any animals residing at the unfinished shelter, Adrian knew that Heather had been making a point of teaching her kids good safety habits.

"Yes, ma'am," Caroline said again. The child was a model of good manners.

Heather shook her head. "That damn dog." Then she reached out and took Adrian's hand. "Come on inside and let me doctor those scratches." She even tugged at his hand to tow him into the building as if he were one of her kids.

And he let her do it, without hesitation.

Chapter 2

HEATHER'S HEART FLUTTERED WHEN SHE WALKED INTO THE shelter's reception area with Adrian's long, strong fingers wrapped around hers. She had grabbed his hand without thinking, but the second their palms connected, an unexpected flash of adrenaline rushed through her. She let go to close the door behind them, then shoved her hands in her pockets.

Reva and Abby came into the room, each holding one end of an extra-large metal crate that they'd set up to house the feral cat. Abby was looking down, struggling to keep her wavy brown hair from falling into her face without letting go of the heavy crate. Short-stepping forward to accommodate Reva's backward steps, Abby looked up and stopped walking. "He doesn't have the cat." She set her end of the crate down.

Reva, who couldn't see them standing behind her, spoke to Abby. "But the cat said—"

"Nope." Abby shook her head. "You were wrong."

Reva eased her side of the crate down on the polished-wood floor, then turned to look. Her shoulders drooped. "Oh. What happened?"

"Jasper happened," Heather said with exasperation. "I'm sorry."

Reva shook her head. "Poor cat. How scared he must have been." The unspoken worry: They'd never be able to catch him after this. He would be much more wary from now on. "Jasper didn't hurt him, did he?"

"No. Jasper's a big goofball who wants cats to stand still so he can get to know them. He just doesn't know how to go about making new friends."

Reva nodded, but her mouth was tight, disappointment clear in her expressive hazel-green eyes. "We'll have to work on that. Apparently, Georgia needs a refresher course in manners around cats as well."

The twins blasted through the front door. "We put Jasper up," Josh yelled, his voice loud in the empty room of hardwood floors and freshly painted taupe walls with white trim. The furniture that had been ordered for the reception area hadn't yet been delivered.

"Thank you," Heather said, lowering her voice in the hope

that her son would also lower his. She didn't want to fuss at him any more than she'd already fussed today (pretty much the whole drive from the elementary school to here). "Would you and Caroline please go get a snack from the fridge?"

Josh's face fell. "But I wanna—"

Caroline took her brother's hand. "Yes, ma'am."

The kids went into the shelter's kitchen, and Heather heard the sounds of Caroline talking quietly to Josh and the refrigerator door being opened. Erin seemed to have disappeared. "Do y'all know where Erin went?"

Reva touched Heather's arm, a gesture of comfort. "She's next door, throwing the ball to Georgia, who has also been banned from the shelter for the rest of the day. Jasper wasn't the only dog who let his baser instincts take over today." Then she looked over at Adrian. "How's your car?"

"I don't know." Adrian made a sound of frustration. "Not good is my guess."

"I'm so sorry," Reva said. "Let me know what I owe you for repairs."

"My insurance will take care of it."

"Well." Reva patted his shoulder. "We'll discuss that later. You need to do something about those scratches so they don't get infected. And after that, we have a meeting to attend."

"I'll finish getting the conference room set up," Abby said. The shelter's conference room had been the dining room of the old house. Reva and Abby had furnished it just last week with an antique Persian rug and a lovely old dining table and matching chairs they'd found at an estate sale. "What should we do with this big ol' crate?"

"Let's leave it set up," Reva said. "Maybe we'll get lucky and catch the cat again soon."

Adrian picked up the crate and set it against the wall where it would be out of the way. Heather tried not to notice the way the muscles in his shoulders and back shifted under his ripped T-shirt. "Reva, would you mind taking the twins next door so Erin can watch them? I'll help Adrian take care of those scratches."

Adrian held up a hand. "No need—"

"Cat scratch fever is a real thing," Reva interrupted in her sternest tone. "And you don't want it. Let Heather help you."

"Yes, ma'am." Adrian's amiable smile made his deep-blue eyes sparkle. He really was too good-looking, if such a thing was possible.

In the kitchen, Reva herded the kids—who were sitting at the kitchen table eating yogurt pops—out the door with the promise of cookies. Heather pointed to the chair

Josh had just vacated. "Sit." She made sure that her voice sounded strong, capable, no-nonsense. "Take off your shirt."

She turned on the faucet, and while the water warmed, she located the first aid bin. She took a washcloth from the drawer next to the sink, filled a big bowl with steaming water, then dropped the cloth in. Before she turned around with the bowl in one hand and the first aid supplies in the other, she steeled herself for what she already knew would be a compelling glimpse of gorgeous man.

Oooh, mama. Her imagination didn't do him justice.

Perched on the chair across from him, she poked through the contents of the first aid box, setting out a bottle of Betadine, a tube of Neosporin, a roll of gauze, and a dispenser of first aid adhesive tape. She wrung out the cloth, then dispensed some Betadine into its folds.

Finally, she met his eyes. Closer than she'd ever been to him before, she noticed that one of his dark-blue eyes had a chocolate-brown occlusion across the top third of the iris. Sitting this close, she could see the shadow of his beard beneath the clean-shaved skin of his square jaw and strong chin with a slight cleft in the center. He smiled at her, a gentle, soft smile that brought out the dimples in his lean, tanned cheeks. Then he closed his eyes and leaned forward. "Do your worst," he said. "I can take it."

As gently as she could, she cleaned the scratches then took the bowl to the sink and dumped it. When she turned back, he was watching her, his eyes heavy-lidded, his long dark lashes obscuring the brown spot in his left eye.

She smiled.

He didn't.

He just watched her with that smoldering, sexy gaze.

She felt like a gazelle being studied by a lion. Her cheeks heated.

Snatching the tube of Neosporin off the table, she moved to stand behind Adrian, where she could escape his steady gaze. Her fingers shook as she twisted the lid of the slippery tube.

"You okay back there?" he asked, a hint of laughter in his voice.

She dangled the tube over his shoulder. "I can't get it open."

Wordlessly, he reached back, took it, uncapped it, and plunked it into her outstretched hand. She applied a bead of the medicine to one of the scratches, dragging her fingertip lightly down his bare skin. He shivered.

Now there was nothing but the intimacy of her skin touching his. She smeared the antibiotic cream on the angry red welts, then covered the worst gouges with gauze and tape. Self-sticking bandages would have been easier, but the scratches were too long for those.

She came around to sit in front of him. Keeping her eyes focused on each scratch as she applied the cream, she managed to get through the process without blushing. She finished applying cream to the last remaining wound and reached back for the gauze.

He covered her hand with his, pinning it between his palm and his warm, hairy chest. "That's good enough."

Startled, she knocked the gauze onto the floor. "Huh?" She would've leaned down to grab the gauze—Weren't medical supplies subject to the three-second rule?—but he didn't release her hand.

He kept her hand pressed to his chest. She could feel his steady heartbeat, his slow breaths in and out, his warm skin heating her palm. Her heart started doing that fluttering thing again.

"That tape isn't gonna stick. It's fine to leave it uncovered."

"Oh." She drew her hand back and put it in her lap. "Okay." She realized with a shock that until now, with the exception of a few brief handshakes, she had never touched a man's bare skin—other than her husband's, of course.

No wonder she'd felt so unsettled.

She was still pondering when Adrian leaned in close...

Her fluttering heart flopped over in her chest. Anticipating the kiss, she sat frozen in place, unable to protest or flee when...

He reached past her to take his shirt off the table, then leaned back to slip it over his head. Her lungs started working again about the time his head emerged from the neck of the shirt.

A slow, sexy grin grew slowly out of the knowing smirk on his lips.

Heart hammering, cheeks flaming, her breathing more shredded than his shirt, Heather pushed her chair back and bolted for the bathroom.

━━━━━━

Reva herded Heather's twins through the swing gate between the shelter and Bayside Barn. She left them in her kitchen with a plate of cookies, a pitcher of Kool-Aid, and strict instructions to mind their big sister and stay put. Then she closed the doggie door in the laundry room and told Georgia to stay put too. Georgia had always had a strong desire to play Miss Manners with the cats—and with other dogs—but that trait had gotten out of hand today when she chased the feral cat.

While Reva walked back to the shelter and across the parking lot, she had a telepathic conversation with Georgia, promising to let her out at the end of the workday when the two gates—one drive-through and one walk-through—between the shelter and Bayside Barn had been closed for the night. She also delivered the bad news that Georgia would be denied permission to go back to the shelter until the feral cat had been caught.

Georgia pouted, sending a mental image of herself turning her back and sticking her little nose in the air. Reva had no doubt that Georgia would also choose to sleep on the couch instead of the bed tonight. Fair enough. Bad behavior had consequences.

Reva stood by Adrian's car and assessed the damage. Not as bad as she'd feared; it looked like none of the scratches were deep enough to require a new paint job. She would insist on paying for Adrian to take the car to the dealership and have the scratches buffed out or whatever they did to restore the factory finish. If it was too much to pay out of pocket, her homeowner's insurance would pay, since it was her dog who'd done the deed.

With that settled in her mind, Reva scanned the heavily wooded area on the other side of the chain-link fence. The strip of vine-covered trees and shrubs was dense but not wide because it bordered the road that dead-ended at an old boat launch into the marshy bayous that edged Magnolia Bay. She didn't feel that the cat was hiding in that narrow strip of land. She didn't sense him in the marshland between here and the bay either. She felt that he was somewhere high and dry. Probably across the road in the vacant lot between here and the next block of estates. Or maybe he was hiding across the street from Bayside Barn in the Cat's Claw forest.

"Where are you?" she asked. Closing her eyes, she reached out with her intuitive abilities and imagined the cat's black-and-white face with its amber eyes, its wide, testosterone-muscled cheeks, and its tattered, battle-torn ears. Slowly, his image shifted, showing her mind an image of his entire body, though it was shrouded in darkness. Hiding under something.

No...in something. A dilapidated structure of some kind. There were plenty of those: the fallen-in house that had been consumed by the Cat's Claw vines across the street, the various sheds out back of the aging estates on this road and the next. "Oh, well." She sent a mind message to the cat. "You're safe enough for now. But you'll be safer if you'll let us take care of you."

She leaned against the front bumper of Heather's car (she knew better than to lean against Adrian's beloved hunk of metal) and spent a few more minutes conversing telepathically with the cat. She tried unsuccessfully to assure him that, contrary to his unfortunate experiences today, it would be better for him to come back to the shelter and allow himself to be brought inside than to remain untethered to humans.

She showed images of the inside of the shelter, in particular the upstairs area that would house the shelter cats. He would be the first resident, the first to climb the treelike cat towers, the first to use the cat doors that led into the two-story outdoor play enclosure full of interesting places to play and climb and hide.

No luck, though. In the image he sent of his reaction to all this, he turned his head away from her and licked his paws. He wasn't impressed.

"Well, then," she asked. "What would it take?"

He showed an image of Adrian cradling the cat loosely in his arms.

"Well, all righty then. I'll tell him."

Not wanting to disturb the planning meeting that had

already started, Reva hung around outside the shelter, watering the potted ferns that hung above the white porch railing, then pulling a few weeds that had dared to spring up in the new flowerbeds around the old-growth gardenias.

After a while, she heard the planning committee folks go outside to look at the cats' outdoor play area. She joined the group and stood at the back, listening to Abby's fiancé, Quinn, who was the project's contractor, explain what he'd done so far and what he still had to do.

While Quinn pointed out the way he had attached the cats' two-story play enclosure to the outside of the old house and installed several cat doors in the exterior wall, Reva noticed Abby watching Quinn with a half smile on her face. Reva couldn't help smiling too. Her niece had found a keeper. Quinn was kind, hardworking, and good to Abby. He wasn't hard to look at either; tall and good-looking, with silky light-brown hair that somehow always managed to be a bit too long.

"Quinn," Heather said. "Where's my hose connection going to be?"

"I haven't run that line yet, so you get to choose."

While Quinn and Heather conferred about hose connections and site drainage, Abby told Adrian and Reva about her plans for the enclosure's landscaping and climbing structures. Despite Abby's animated hand gestures, Adrian's gaze kept drifting to Heather, who stood with her back to him, her hands on her curvaceous hips while she nodded at something Quinn was saying. It seemed that Adrian couldn't keep his eyes from lingering on Heather.

"Hmmm," Reva murmured. "Isn't that interesting?"

"Oh, definitely!" Abby agreed. "Not only will it give the cats plenty of enrichment and exercise, it doubles the amount of space they'll have."

"Um-hmm," Reva agreed. But she hadn't been commenting about the cats.

After the meeting broke up, Adrian hung around and talked to Quinn while Reva and Abby went back inside to clean the conference room and lock up. Halfway listening to Quinn, Adrian watched Heather walk through the gate between the shelter and Reva's house to collect her kids.

He really hadn't meant to scare the bejesus out of her by leaning in so close. Yes, he admitted he was teasing her, just a little, by coming in close enough to kiss while reaching for his shirt. She was such an easy mark, though, that it was hard to resist. All he had to do was look at her and lower his eyelids a fraction to get her to blush. He realized too late that he shouldn't have pushed the envelope quite so far. He'd been half-hoping she'd lean in too and invite a kiss for real, but instead, she had jumped up like a scalded cat and rushed out of the room, leaving him to clean up the mess from her Florence Nightingale routine.

Only fair, he supposed.

Next time, he'd be more aware of her subtle cues. He had only wanted to flirt, not to embarrass her. She hadn't met his eyes since the almost-kiss; for the entire meeting and the site tour that followed, she'd managed not to look at him.

He figured that hiding back here with Quinn until Heather left would save her further embarrassment and that by next week's meeting, she'd be over it. He'd thought about apologizing, but (a) that might make things worse, and (b) he wasn't sorry he'd invited an opportunity for kissing. If anyone needed kissing in a bad way, it was Heather. That woman was wound tighter than Dick's hatband.

"See?" Quinn was saying. "We subdivided the existing three-car garage into kennels and added a doggie door on the exterior wall of each one. Every kennel will have a separate chain-link dog run and 24/7 access to the outdoors. Heather says that'll cut down on cleaning. And Reva says it'll provide natural house-training for the dogs because they'd rather do their business outside if they can."

"That's genius," Adrian said.

A second later, he was tackled from behind. He stumbled but managed to stay upright as Josh grabbed his hand and walked up his jeans. What had seemed, at first, to be a good attempt at a run-up-the-wall back flip ended with Adrian's shoulder possibly out of joint and Josh rolling in a giggling heap on the ground, leaving red-dirt footprints as high up as Adrian's hip.

"Josh!" Heather ran toward them, her eyes wide with alarm. "What are you doing?" She snatched her son up by the arm. Adrian tried not to look at her heaving bosom as she spoke to her son in a curiously firm tone for such a soft voice. "That was not okay."

Quinn put his hands up. "Uh-oh. Family drama. I think I hear Abby calling me."

Quinn quickly absconded, brushing past Erin and Caroline, who were standing behind Heather.

"Erin, please go get Jasper out of the kennel and put him in the car." The five-star-general aspect of Heather's personality emerged, apparently banishing her embarrassment more effectively than anything Adrian could have done to talk her out of it. "Caroline, please go with your sister and close all the gates securely behind you. Josh, please stand exactly where you are and tell Mr. Crawford how sorry you are that you ambushed him."

Erin and Caroline went off in the direction of the kennels, and Josh looked up at his mother, innocently blinking his wide blue eyes. "What's 'ambushed' mean?"

That didn't cut it with Heather. "I will show you how to look the word up in the dictionary when we get home. And to make sure you remember the meaning, I'll get you to write it down five or ten times. Now. You know what you did, and you know it was wrong. Please apologize." The unspoken threat behind her polite wording hovered in the air.

Josh looked down at his feet and drew a line in the clay-rich red dirt that had been hauled in to level the construction site outside the existing buildings. "I'm sorry," he mumbled.

Heather crossed her arms. "I'm not sure anyone heard you, and when you apologize, you are supposed to look the person in the eye and say what you're sorry for. Let's try that again."

Adrian knew how excruciating this kind of chastisement in front of others would feel to any kid, much less one who wasn't yet knee-high to a grasshopper. And he owed something to Heather after taking his natural tendency to flirt a little too far.

He knelt down in front of Josh. "It's okay. I know you didn't mean anything by it. But your mother is right. When you…" He struggled to find a small enough word for *accost*, *invade*, *violate*. "When you sneak up on someone without their permission, it's…" Shit fire; again, he struggled to come up with a ten-cent word to explain a five-dollar concept. "It's a… It's a *good thing* to apologize."

Josh looked down at his feet, continuing to scrub lines in the dirt with the toe of his shoe.

"Josh…" Heather said in a warning tone.

Adrian held out both hands, and Josh grabbed hold. Adrian squeezed the kid's fingers lightly, giving encouragement. "I'm right here, and I'm not mad. Just say what you need to say, and I promise, it'll be fine."

"Um…" Josh's voice shook, then faltered.

Adrian looked down at the boy's short little fingers clutching his much longer ones. Josh's hands were so small, still bearing the marks of babyhood in the dimples above each knuckle. Adrian looked up into Josh's ice-blue eyes that he must have gotten from his father. "It's okay, buddy," Adrian said, even though it seemed that the hint of understanding he showed made the kid's bottom lip tremble with emotion.

Josh clutched Adrian's hands and stared into his eyes. "I'm sorry, Mister..." He glanced up at Heather, obviously unable to remember Adrian's surname, since he'd probably only heard it this once.

"Hey." Adrian brought Josh's attention back to him. "You know what? You can call me Ade, like Quinn does, because he's my buddy from way back. We can dispense with the Mister."

Josh's blond brows drew together for a second while he looked off to the side (probably wondering about the word *dispense*); then he looked into Adrian's eyes again. "I'm sorry I sneaked up on you and climbed up your legs." The words tumbled out in a rush, and then he leaned close and whispered into Adrian's ear. "I hope I didn't hurt you. I didn't, did I?"

Adrian patted Josh's back. "No," he said quietly. "You didn't hurt me."

"I'm glad." Josh's small body relaxed in relief. "I wasn't thinking." He wrapped his arms around Adrian's neck and held on. "I was just so happy you were still here so I could say goodbye before we left."

Adrian's heart cracked open at the kid's raw honesty. A kid, he realized, who hadn't been able to say a last goodbye to his father because Dale had died so suddenly that goodbyes weren't possible. Nobody had ever mentioned to Adrian what, exactly, had happened to Dale, and Adrian hadn't felt comfortable asking for details that weren't given freely. He only knew from talking to Quinn and Abby and Reva that Dale's death was so unexpected and upsetting that the whole family was still struggling with PTSD along with their grief.

Heather reached down to touch Josh's shoulder. "That was a good apology, Joshua. I'm proud of you."

Josh nodded, then pulled away from Adrian just far enough to look at him. "I'm glad you're okay." His face brightened. "You want to come to dinner? My mom cooks great."

"Maybe one of these days." Adrian smiled at Josh, then chanced a look at Heather. Her pink lips were curved in a soft smile.

"You could come tonight," Josh insisted. "Friday is spaghetti night. Mama makes toasty cheese bread then. And salad, but you don't have to eat it if you don't want to. *I* have to at least try it, but she won't make you do that."

"Josh," Heather said softly. "I have a Zoom meeting with

Sara tonight so we can prepare for Monday's PTA meeting. And we need to get going."

"Well, when *can* he come?" Josh asked, a mulish expression on his face.

Heather blushed. "I don't know, Josh. We'll have to figure that out later."

"Promise?" Josh whined. He sent an imploring look to Heather, then to Adrian. "Do y'all promise you'll figure it out?"

Heather sighed heavily. "I promise. Now let's go. I can't be late for the meeting, and I still have to cook your dinner."

Josh looked back at Adrian. "You promise too? You'll come to dinner? Soon?"

Adrian tried to give Josh a reassuring smile, but it felt pasted on. Family dinner night at Heather's was a fate he hoped to avoid. He was happy to flirt—and to follow that wherever it led—but he didn't want to put down roots. He had to say something though, and making idle promises didn't sit right. "I'll try."

It was the best he could do, and even that felt like too much commitment.

He stood and received Josh's fervent hug.

Heather blushed. "Sorry about all this." She took Josh's

hand and urged him to take two steps in the direction of the car, even though he reached out for Adrian dramatically; a brilliant career in the theater definitely awaited. She dragged her son another few staggering steps. "See you next Friday, Adrian."

"I'll be here." He watched the struggle, almost halfway wishing he could help, but mostly glad he didn't have to.

Erin and Caroline led Jasper through the gate from the kennels to the parking lot, and Heather stooped down to get her son's attention. "We really do have to go now. Please say goodbye, Josh."

"Goodbye, Josh," the kid mimicked with a silly, clownish look on his face. Unlike his twin sister, Josh was not a wilting flower. But it was clear that his manic appeal for attention covered deep insecurity and sadness.

Adrian waved, his face carefully expressionless. "See you next week." Because his presence seemed to ignite Josh's veering emotions, Adrian turned back toward the shelter, planning to hide out of sight by the kennels until Heather left, then hightail it to his car and get the hell out of Dodge.

———————

That evening, when Heather and the kids got home from the meeting at the shelter, she couldn't help noticing Charlie,

Dale's lonely and pitiful horse, standing alone in the field behind the house with his head low. With his head down like that, the retired racehorse—who had loved nothing more than to run like the wind with Dale on his back—was reduced to a sad brown blob of misery in the distance.

She wondered for the millionth time whether they should get Charlie a goat or a donkey for company, but it wasn't fair to ask Erin to take on even more responsibility. She already had to feed the poor thing, scoop his stall out every evening, and deep-clean his stall every weekend. Dale had done those jobs because Charlie had been his horse, but Charlie, like everyone else in the family, had lived a diminished existence ever since Dale died.

"Erin," she said as they sat in the car and waited for the garage door to creak open. "Please go out to the barn and take care of Charlie before you do anything else, okay?"

"Dammit, Mom," Erin groused. "I have a ton of homework to do."

"And the whole weekend to do it," Heather replied, ignoring the fact that Erin had just said *dammit*. There were some arguments she didn't have the strength for, and right this minute, Erin's little outburst was one of them.

Heather parked the car in the garage and got out before

her temptation to be a better mother got the best of her. It was fine, she told herself, to let Erin's bad language slide, just this once. "Get all your stuff out of the car," she said over her shoulder. "I don't want any Monday-morning hysteria about not being able to find something you left in the car."

In the kitchen, Caroline and Josh fed the dog while Heather set a pot of salted water and a skillet on the stove. Erin hefted her backpack onto the granite-topped island then slammed out the door on her way to feed Charlie Horse.

Heather thought about the weeks she and Dale had spent picking out that countertop when they built this house. They'd gone to every granite store in the state of Louisiana (and a few in Mississippi) until they found a beautiful slab in the subdued browns and grays Dale could live with that also contained the interesting striations of silver and crystal formations she insisted upon.

Everything, everything—from the distressed-leather wall treatment she had chosen to the unimaginative white ceilings and trim she'd let him have—everything reminded her of him. And every time she noticed or remembered anything about the building of this house, she sent up a prayer of thanks that Dale had insisted on buying more life insurance than she'd thought they could afford.

Dale's life insurance had paid off the house and covered the bills for a year so she could continue being a stay-at-home mom. That gift had allowed her to keep their lives as consistent as possible. Taking a job would change a lot, but at least they could afford to keep living here.

Heather sighed and went back to smashing the browning ground beef and seasoned sausage in the skillet into ever more tiny chunks. The time of respite and recovery she had resolved to give herself and her kids was now over, and time continued to march onward.

Dale's birthday would have been next Wednesday. The first missed birthday after Dale died came when they were all still shell-shocked, so the kids hadn't remembered. This time, though, they might. Heather wondered if she should plan something to commemorate the date—maybe a visit to the cemetery followed by a special dinner.

Jasper nosed her leg, looking for a handout, his little stub tail wagging. She handed him a chunk of cooked carrot, which she'd been chopping finely enough to hide in the spaghetti sauce. He took it from her fingers so gently that it warmed her heart.

Jasper nosed her leg again. "Ever hopeful," she said to his pleading brown-and-blue-marbled eyes. She gave him another carrot and stroked the whirlwind-shaped cowlick in the middle of the white blaze at the bridge of his nose.

Aside from the cowlick, Jasper was a perfectly marked red merle Australian Shepherd. The pure-white blaze that started at the tip of his nose went up his forehead to widen between his ears and join up with the ruff around his neck. His feet and legs had white socks edged in copper, and the rest of his thick wavy coat was speckled in shades from the lightest honey to the darkest brown.

"You're gonna like working at the shelter, aren't you, Jasper?"

The dog panted, smiling. Always happy, always spreading joy. Jasper was actually one of the reasons Heather had decided to take the job at the shelter. Where else could she work that would allow her to bring her kids *and* the dog?

The only fly in her ointment at the shelter was Adrian Crawford and her conflicted feelings toward him. Because sometimes, when she noticed him looking at her with those deep, dark midnight-blue eyes or when he brushed past her with his overtly masculine presence (because even in those leather loafers he wore sometimes, there was no denying his masculinity), she would remember that she wasn't just Dale's widow; she was a woman.

And every time it happened—those little wisps of connection that clung to her skin like strands of spiderweb for hours afterward—she felt as guilty as if she'd just woken from an erotic but disturbing dream in which she had cheated on Dale.

Her husband, the love of her life, was gone. She knew that it wasn't possible to cheat on a dead man. But her newly awakening womanhood felt as uncomfortable as the pins-and-needles feeling of a gone-to-sleep limb whose circulation was just beginning to flow again. In a way, it felt good. But it also hurt, maybe more than she could bear.

Chapter 3

ADRIAN SAT ACROSS FROM QUINN IN THE HOT TUB AT REVA'S house and gazed out over the green pastures that rolled out behind Bayside Barn and eventually led to the marsh-lined bay.

Quinn leaned back and sighed. "Glad you decided to stay a while."

"Your offer of a cold beer by the hot tub was hard to argue with."

Reva and Abby stepped onto the patio with their hands full. Reva set a couple of hors d'oeuvre plates on the edge of the hot tub, while Abby handed out Stella Artois to the guys and wine to the ladies. Abby sat beside Quinn, then Reva sat between the two men and held her wineglass out for a toast. "I'm so glad you agreed to stay a bit longer before heading home."

"Me too." Adrian joined in the toast and took a sip, then set his bottle aside. "Thanks for the invite."

"Mind that bottle," Reva warned. "Georgia will knock it over if it gets between her and the tennis ball."

Quinn hurled Georgia's ball into the gathering darkness beyond the patio lights. Georgia took off like a bullet after it. "Yeah, she will," he agreed. "She's obsessed."

"I'll be careful." Adrian could see how the combo of Georgia's game of fetch and glass bottles might be a problem. The hot tub and the pool were built-in level with the patio slab and within easy reach of the super-focused cattle dog mix who clearly cared about nothing but playing ball.

Wolf, the elusive wolf hybrid who'd chosen Quinn as his person, sat at the edge of the patio where the solar lights met the clipped-grass lawn. He seemed to care nothing about chasing the ball and everything about guarding everyone within his domain.

"Dinner's in the oven for those who are staying," Reva said. "And, Adrian, I won't insist, though the invitation remains open." She reached for one of the hors d'oeuvre plates and drew it closer. "But meanwhile, this should keep your stomach from thinking your throat's been cut."

"Disturbingly morbid," Quinn said.

Adrian wasn't sure whether his friend was talking about Reva's comment or the serving dish. He helped himself to one of the toothpicks that stuck out of a sculpted mummy in the center of the dish, then stabbed a tiny sausage.

"Grayson and I found these serving dishes at some hole-in-the-wall shop in the French Quarter. Can't remember where, though. It was years ago." Reva's voice didn't sound sad, but Adrian felt her sadness all the same. She and Heather were both widows—that was how they'd met, at a grief support group—and even though they were both cheerful and upbeat on the surface, there still seemed to be an invisible, protective cloak of sadness around them.

Big reason—the biggest—why Adrian kept reminding himself to stay away from Heather. Even though he regularly managed to forget the fact that flirting with Heather was flirting with fire. He wasn't averse to some level of commitment to the right woman, preferably someone as driven and success-minded as himself. But Heather was a whirlpool of unacknowledged needs that he could too easily get sucked into if he let himself get too close. And now that he'd witnessed firsthand how messed-up Josh was...

Georgia brought the ball back to Quinn and dropped it a

hair too close to the snack tray. Abby grabbed the ball and dropped it into the hot tub. "Done playing, girl."

Clearly not convinced the game was over, the dog dropped to the ground and eyed the ball.

Adrian looked at Reva as she sipped her wine. Probably about the same age as Adrian's mother, Reva was young-looking and beautiful, her shiny hair silver-gray but lush and long and pulled back in a barrette.

Conversation circulated above the bubbles in the hot tub. But Adrian was thinking about the differences between Reva and his mother, who, while still attractive, looked older and more matronly than Reva. Adrian's parents' example of what not to do was another reason he needed to keep a distance from Heather.

Gordon and Eileen Crawford were still in love after however many years, but they had each given up many of their goals and dreams in order to stay together.

Even after Hurricane Katrina, when Adrian's parents and younger siblings had moved back into the rebuilt family home, Eileen had prevented Gordon from taking promotions that would've required them to move, just as he had prevented her from going back to school and getting a degree once their kids were grown.

Maybe Hurricane Katrina had been a blessing in disguise, at least for Adrian. Though the storm had torn through his relationships, washed away opportunities, and trashed his senior year in high school, the complete derailing of his life at such a pivotal time had changed him and shifted his priorities. Adrian's potentially glorious senior year of high school had been sucked up by the storm. He'd lost his girlfriend and the college scholarship that had been all but promised to him as the star quarterback of his high school football team.

He'd lost everything he thought he wanted and become a castaway in a big city where he knew no one—other than his college-age cousin, who'd been forced by his parents to give Adrian a place to sleep but was under no obligation to make him feel welcome.

It hadn't been easy, but Adrian had learned how to take care of himself and depend on no one.

Every disappointment had been followed by a lesson that made him better off in the long run. He'd become successful by learning not to want or expect anything from anyone other than himself.

Adrian didn't want to be in the kind of relationship that caused both partners to get beaten down by life. And the only way he knew to avoid that was to avoid falling in love.

Luckily, that wasn't difficult. He had perfected the art of enjoying close relationships while still keeping his distance.

"Adrian," Reva said, "can I get you another beer?"

"No thanks. I'm good." He'd be driving back home to New Orleans—just an hour from here—soon.

A low, moaning yowl in the distance escalated into a hair-raising scream. Adrian sat forward and looked out over the rolling hills behind Reva's house and the big red barn. But all he could see was a gorgeous violet-streaked sky over the bay that glittered just beyond the fenced pastures. Another, deeper yowl echoed from a different location nearby. "What in the hell was that?"

"Feral tomcats," Reva said.

"You think one of them is the black-and-white one I caught today?"

"Pretty certain of it," Reva answered. "That's why I was so disappointed when you didn't manage to hold on to him."

"We've been trying to trap both of them," Abby added. "But those old tomcats are wily. They know better than to be fooled by the smell of canned tuna."

Quinn chuckled. "I think the cats around here have told them they'll be relieved of their testicles if they fall for the old tuna-in-a-trap trick."

"We've caught a bunch of raccoons though," Reva said. "I think at least a few of them were disappointed when we let them go. They wouldn't have minded a small surgical procedure if it led to a lifetime of luxury."

The yowls and screams eventually clashed in the crescendo of a truly vicious-sounding cat fight. "How far away do you think they are?"

"Sounds carry a long way around here," Quinn said. "We can easily hear boats on the bay, and it's, what? A mile down the hill?"

"That depends on whether you count the marsh between here and the bay as land or water," Reva answered. "But yes, it's about a mile from here to the bay."

"The sound carries, though," Abby said, "because there's not much to absorb it. Just the marsh grass and that big oak tree in the pasture."

The catfight broke up, and the sound of crickets and bubbling water took over again. "That sounded seriously violent," Adrian said. "I wonder if they both walked away."

"Yeah," Reva said. "They probably left a significant amount of fur on the ground, though." Her phone chirped, and she stood. "That's my cue to check on dinner and make the salad, which gives everyone about a half hour before it's time to mosey back inside."

"Need any help?" Abby asked.

"No, thanks. Y'all finish your drinks and come on in when you're ready. Adrian, even if you decide not to stay for dinner, I hope you'll come inside and say goodbye before you leave. There's something I want to give you."

Nobody else jumped up, so Adrian relaxed and enjoyed his beer. The violet-and-lavender sky turned to pearl gray, and a few stars emerged in its cotton-soft depths. The little pond under the oak tree glowed dimly with reflected light. "It's peaceful here," Adrian decided out loud.

"Catfights notwithstanding," Quinn agreed. "Not quite so peaceful during school days, though. I'm not looking forward to the beginning of field trip season."

Abby put a hand on Quinn's shoulder and patted lightly—a there-there-honey pat. "Field trips will be few and far between until October."

Adrian knew that Bayside Barn was a field trip destination for schoolkids as far away as New Orleans. It was essentially a petting zoo, though Reva and Abby used a more highfalutin term: animal-assisted education center.

"Thank God we've nearly completed the Great Wall of

China between the shelter and here," Quinn's description wasn't much of an exaggeration. What had once been a hedge-covered chain-link fence between the two properties was now a nine-foot-tall concrete-block wall. The imposing edifice was broken only by a sliding drive-through gate and a smaller walk-through gate.

"If you hadn't gone so far overboard on that wall, it'd be long since done by now," Abby said to her fiancé with a slight tone of I-told-you-so in her voice.

Quinn scoffed. "It'll be worth it. Kids screaming and yelling next door all day every day couldn't possibly be good for the shelter animals' mental and emotional health."

Now it was Abby's turn to scoff. "Yours, you mean. Funny, since we'll be living on the Bayside Barn side of the fence once the shelter opens."

"Only until after the wedding," Quinn said. "Then we'll start looking for our own place."

Abby gave Quinn another there-there pat. "Whatever you want. Meanwhile, we'll have fun playing house in the little cabin you're building behind Bayside Barn."

The lovebirds weren't kissing or even sitting up against each other, but without Reva's balancing presence, Adrian started feeling claustrophobic. "Welp..." He finished his beer in one gulp. "It's been fun, y'all." He stood and wrapped a towel around his waist. "But I really need to get home."

He changed into his clothes in the guest bathroom at Reva's house, leaving the towel and borrowed swim trunks hanging on the shower curtain bar. Then he found Reva in the kitchen, where she stood with her back to him, fiddling with something on the counter.

"I'm about to head out," he said.

She turned around with a covered dish in her hand. "For you to heat up later."

"Thanks." He took the warm container. "I'm glad I stayed to visit. I enjoyed it."

"I hope you'll hang out with us after these shelter meetings more often. You have a standing invitation." She linked her arm in his. "Let me walk you out."

"There's no need."

"I have to lock the gates anyway." She took a flashlight off a hook by the door and led the way from Bayside Barn to the shelter. "I also wanted to talk to you about that cat."

"What about him?"

"He seems to have bonded with you." She opened the gate between the dogs' play yards and the parking lot, then held it open for him. "I believe that he will come to you again if you work to regain his trust. Would you be willing to do that?"

Adrian walked beside Reva toward his car, its black surface appearing gunmetal gray in the glow of the flashlight's beam. "What exactly does *work to regain his trust* mean?"

"I know it's asking a lot."

"Just ask. I can always say no." Though he hadn't been very good at that lately.

"I know you've been donating your time for this shelter project once a week. But if you could see your way to come more often, maybe twice a week—just for an hour or two each time—he'd sense your presence, and he'd be more likely to come back to you. You could call out to him, leave treats by your car, let him know you want to make a connection with him."

"I don't see why I'm the one who needs to do this. What makes me so special?"

"You're special to all of us for helping us get this project off the ground." She patted his arm in a motherly fashion. "But there's something about you that makes this cat feel safe. I don't know what it is, but I think that together, we can figure it out. I think we need to try before he gets hurt more than he already has been."

Adrian had noticed the cat's many injuries.

And hell, it wasn't like Adrian couldn't spare the time. He worked from home 90 percent of the time. He could bring his laptop, pull up a chair, and sit by this fence a few hours a week without it touching his bottom line. Even the hour-long drive here and back wouldn't be wasted because he could use the time to make phone calls from the car.

"Okay, fine." He took the keys from his jeans pocket and clicked the unlock button. "I'll be here Wednesday afternoon."

＝＝＝＝＝＝

Heather woke just before dawn on the morning of Dale's birthday and watched the sky outside her bedroom window lighten from gray to lavender to pearly pink to pale blue. Though she had made plans to commemorate the occasion in the afternoon, she resolved not to tell the kids that today was anything special until then. The twins definitely wouldn't remember the date, and Heather hoped Erin wouldn't either. Heather didn't want a sense of loss to sabotage their school day.

The plan, Heather decided, was to drop everyone off at school, then make a grocery store run to get a birthday cake—that wasn't weird, was it?—for the family to share after dinner as a way of remembrance. After school, they'd stop by the cemetery to put fresh flowers on Dale's grave. If everyone felt okay afterward, they might swing by the animal shelter on the way home, just to see how things were going. It would be fine. They'd get through the day together. And maybe next year, it wouldn't be so hard.

Luckily, the kids didn't notice anything different about the morning, and the school drop-off happened without a hitch. Jasper's feelings were hurt when he didn't get to come along. But the summer heat didn't allow him to wait in the car while Heather shopped, so he had to be left behind. Erin exited the car with a breezy goodbye, and five minutes later, Heather waved goodbye to the twins.

She turned up the volume on her *Happy Music* Spotify playlist and sang along to "Don't Worry, Be Happy." The gaiety was forced, sure. But fake-it-till-you-make-it was a baked-in component of her personality. She had made the cheerleading squad that way. She had started out her adult life that way, masquerading as an adult until she became one. And when Dale died, she pretended to be able to cope until she figured out a way to cope for real.

That afternoon, when Heather parked outside the middle

school, Erin was one of the first kids out the door. She breezed up to the car and hopped in, tossing her backpack on the floor. "Hey, Mom." Leaning across the seat, she kissed Heather's cheek, then buckled her seat belt. "How was your day?"

"Fine, thanks." Heather merged into the line of cars leaving the school. "You look happy today."

"I got invited to join the yearbook club. They're meeting at Sierra's house tonight; she said her mom would pick me up and bring me back home after."

"Oh." Heather hoped Erin's opportunity didn't interfere with her afternoon plans. "What time?"

"Five. They'll have pizza, so I won't have to eat first."

Cutting it close, but still doable. "That's wonderful, sweetie." They would still have time to go by the cemetery. She drove a few more miles debating how to break the news that they'd be going to visit Dale's grave today. She wasn't sure why she expected a blowup from Erin, but she did. Better to get it over with before the twins got out of school. "I have a surprise for you too."

Erin looked up from her phone with an excited smile. "Yeah?"

"After we pick up the twins, we're going to have a special little celebration, just the four of us."

"What are we celebrating?"

Heather took a breath. "Today's your daddy's birthday, so I thought—"

Erin drew back as if she'd been slapped. "We're...celebrating? Mom, that makes absolutely no sense."

"I thought—"

"I was having a great day, the first great day I've had in *ages*, and you just had to go and ruin it, didn't you?" Erin's cheeks stained red with anger. "You can't stand that I'm happy. I'm finally just a regular kid at school, not *that girl whose daddy just died*." She flung up her hands. "Daddy is *dead*, Mom. Get over it already."

"Well...but..." Heather sputtered. She had expected some grumbling from Erin, but not such a vitriolic attack. "I thought it would be nice to commemorate his birthday. It's not a big deal."

"It's not? Well, good." Erin flounced around in her seat, crossed her arms, and stared out the window. "Because I don't want any part of it. You and the twins can do whatever stupid thing you've cooked up, but you can take me straight home. I need to take a shower and change clothes and get ready for tonight."

Heather clutched the steering wheel. Dale would've

probably pulled the car over and...well, she didn't know what he would've done because Erin had never stood up to either of them the way she'd done just now. But Dale would have known how to handle it. Heather didn't. Should she force Erin to go along? That would ruin the whole afternoon for everyone and defeat the purpose of remembering Dale in this small and meaningful way. But if she let Erin stay home, she would be rewarding a tantrum. "It won't take more than an hour..."

Erin cut a sideways look of fury toward Heather before responding. "I have homework to do too."

Heather felt a headache begin to throb behind her left eye, and she realized that her teeth were clenched, her shoulders tensed, her whole body geared up for a confrontation. She forced herself to relax.

She drove the rest of the way to the elementary school in silence. Erin fumed silently, her fingers flying on her phone's touch screen. Probably texting a friend to say how horribly she was being treated.

Outside Magnolia Bay Elementary School's red-brick building, the twins piled into the back seat. Caroline sat quietly and buckled her seat belt, while Josh filled the car with his loud chatter and the smell of little-boy sweat and playground dirt. Erin sighed, rolled her eyes, and took a pair of headphones from her backpack, pointedly plugging herself into her phone.

At that moment, Heather decided to take Erin home. Then she could talk to the twins without Erin's argumentative presence tainting the conversation. She reminded herself that her intention was to make a new family ritual that would help the kids remember Dale in ways that cemented good memories and made even more good memories going forward. Forcing any of them to participate would only accomplish the exact opposite. Erin was old enough to remember Dale; the twins were the ones who most needed those memories to be nurtured into the future.

When they got to the house, Erin slammed out of the car and stormed toward the house before any of the others had even shifted in their seats.

"Hang on, kids," Heather said. "I want to talk to y'all a second."

She explained her plan for the afternoon and the reason for it. Then, instead of telling them they had to come along—because making Erin babysit while Heather went by herself would be a nice bit of passive-aggressive poetic justice—she let them decide for themselves.

"Sure," Josh said. "I want to go. Can we get ice cream too?"

Caroline bounced in her seat. "Yes, please, but can I go inside and pee first?"

"Sure, honey." Heather cut the engine. "Let's all go in for a few minutes before we leave."

Heather knocked lightly before opening the door to Erin's room. It wasn't quite a pigsty but wasn't far from it either. Erin had flung herself onto the messy bed, clearly prepared to sulk whether she got her way or not. "You told me you cleaned your room this past weekend."

"I did." Erin's voice was muffled by the mattress. "It got dirty again."

"I see." Heather waited a few seconds, but Erin didn't say anything else. "Well, the twins and I are going to the cemetery, and you are welcome to change your mind and come along if you'd like."

Erin shook her head and mumbled something.

"Suit yourself." Heather closed Erin's door softly and walked away.

━━━━━━━━━━

Charlie stood in the field and watched the family's car drive away again, though it had only been in the garage for a few minutes. Charlie's people spent a lot of time coming and going but very little time interacting with him. He understood; he didn't deserve their time or attention.

He stood with his nose to the ground, though he wasn't grazing. His belly hurt, so he hadn't eaten this morning, but Erin didn't know that because she always poured his daily scoop of sweetened oats into the bin without looking. He hadn't eaten the hay that she'd tossed into the hayrack in the corner of his stall either. He had torn at it in frustration, so most of it got scattered on top of his droppings or stuck to the peed-on mass of wood shavings that squished under his hooves.

Dale had always made sure that Charlie had a fluffy layer of shavings to stomp through and to lie on at night if he decided to relax fully instead of sleeping standing up. But Erin rarely took the time to scrape the stall down to the bare-dirt floor before adding fresh bedding. The substrate of Charlie's stall was often so soaked with urine that it irritated his skin if he decided to lie down to sleep. He had always tried to avoid messing in his own stall, but sometimes Erin put him up too early in the afternoons. And when that happened, he just couldn't help making a mess.

Life after Dale wasn't really worth living.

No more than Charlie deserved, he knew.

He hadn't meant to do it.

A hot breeze blew across the pasture, sending tufts of milkweed tumbling across the too-tall alfalfa grass.

Dale had kept the pasture mowed-down so the blades Charlie nibbled were always juicy and sweet. Ever since Charlie had killed the person he loved most in the world, the grasses and weeds had been left to grow tall and bitter.

Charlie hadn't meant to do it.

But that didn't matter.

Nothing did. If Charlie had known how to will himself to die, he would have done it already. Maybe now that his belly hurt so much that he couldn't bring himself to eat, the release he longed for would finally happen.

━━━━━━━━

When Adrian got to the shelter that afternoon, he laughed out loud at the sight that greeted him. He pulled into his usual parking spot next to a folding chair and tiny worktable with an even tinier ice chest on top. He hadn't confirmed that he would actually show up to help tame the feral cat, but apparently, Reva had faith in him.

He put his phone and laptop on the table, then covered his

car with the tarp. When he opened the ice chest, he laughed again. "Thanks, Reva," he said out loud, popping the top on a cold beer. He took a swig and poked through the contents nestled into a bed of ice. A bottle of water, a baggie of sesame sticks in a paper bowl (for him, he assumed), and another baggie... He turned it over to read the label written with a Sharpie in flowing longhand: *Kitty Crack*. And, in another baggie, a small squirt bottle of citronella bug spray.

He set his beer on the table and settled in to begin the campaign to lure the feral tomcat to his eventual fate as a domesticated house cat. "Better you than me, dude," he said to the cat who was still nowhere to be seen. "Here, kitty, kitty."

After opening his laptop and connecting to the shelter's Wi-Fi, he clicked on an email, then tossed a cat treat through the fence and into the tangle of trees beyond. "Well, shit." That was stupid. He tossed the next one with a little less oomph. It bounced on the gravel and through the fence, landing a couple of inches from the wire. "Better."

He dealt with emails, calling, "Here, kitty, kitty," every now and again. Ten emails later, his relative inattention was rewarded; Stinky Cat sat hunched on the other side of the fence, crunching on the Kitty Crack. "Hey, buddy." Adrian threw another morsel. "What's up in the big, bad world?"

The cat declined to answer—or even to look up. He crept over to the new treat and started munching, so Adrian threw another few treats, this time making sure some of them landed on his side of the fence. Reva came across the parking lot carrying a small cat crate. "How's it going?"

Adrian leaned back in the folding chair. "As you see. That crate might be a little premature."

Reva set the crate down next to the fence, several yards down from Adrian's impromptu office space. "I'm setting this up for later to get him used to the crate." Reva propped the crate's open door against the fence and set a plastic container of food inside. "Also, I just got a text from Heather. She and the twins are on their way here." She stood slowly. The tomcat looked up but kept eating the treat he was working on. "I thought I'd let you know in case you were thinking of picking up the cat. I wouldn't want you to get flayed alive again."

"They're bringing that horrible dog, I take it."

"Not this time. They're... They've just left the cemetery. Today was Dale's birthday. Apparently, the visit to the gravesite didn't go as planned."

This was precisely the sort of shit Adrian didn't want to get involved in, but it seemed that a response was expected. "Oh?"

"Heather was hoping it would be a...celebration of sorts, but it didn't turn out that way."

He snorted. "No shit."

Reva narrowed her eyes at him. "Be nice."

Chastised, he retreated behind his charming half smile. "Yes, ma'am."

She drifted closer, her arms crossed. The cat looked up but didn't move. "I'm going to take the kids across to Bayside Barn and get them involved in feeding critters. Take their minds off missing their dad."

"Sounds like a plan." Adrian closed his laptop, since Reva was distracting him from finishing his emails anyway. Maybe he'd head home earlier than he'd planned. The cat wouldn't cross the fence until all the coming and going had stopped for the day, so he was officially wasting his time now. "I guess I'll—"

"I was hoping," Reva cut him off, "that you'd talk with Heather. Maybe go for a walk or something. Cheer her up a little."

"I've actually got a lot of work to..." His voice drifted off in the face of Reva's disapproving expression. With her crossed arms and her pursed lips, she reminded him a lot of his mother right this minute. "Um...I really do have a bit of work to do still." He wasn't lying; once he finished with emails, he had to edit a draft business plan for a new startup company he was advising.

But Reva's silent stare was scarier even than his mom's. "I guess I could...um...spare a few minutes before I head home."

Reva's pursed lips stayed pursed, and her squinting eyes stayed squinted. She tightened her crossed arms.

"Maybe I'll take her for a quick spin in the convertible."

Reva smiled and patted his shoulder. "That's a wonderful idea. I'm so glad you thought of it."

─────────────

Heather arrived at the shelter with two very subdued kids in the back seat. Maybe Erin had been right after all. Heather needed to stop living in the past and allow Dale's shadow to fade away.

She parked near the shelter's front porch, and Reva opened the back door for the twins. "Hey, you guys," Reva said with excitement to the kids who crawled out of the car. "You want to come see the baby bunnies?"

Caroline nodded soberly, her thumb still in her mouth.

"I guess so," Josh answered, sounding sullen and unhappy.

"Come on then." Reva held out her hands. "You can help me feed the barn critters too."

Heather got out of the car, feeling lost. She needed a hug, but Reva's attention was all on the twins. Reva tipped a chin toward the far end of the lot, where Adrian was folding the canvas tarp and putting it in the trunk of his car. "Go see that one. Ask him how the cat taming is going. No talking—or even thinking—about you-know-who allowed."

She looked over at Adrian. "I don't think he wants to be bothered with me and my problems."

"I'm sure he doesn't. So don't bother him. Just go somewhere and have fun. He'll be able to remind you how that's done, in case you've forgotten."

Heather shook her head but schlepped across the parking lot toward Adrian, who had climbed into his low-slung car and started the engine. The automatic convertible top started folding back all by itself. "Fancy," she said when she drew even with the passenger door.

"Of course," he replied with a wink and a grin. "Get in."

She hesitated a moment, glancing to where Reva had taken the kids, but then got in and slammed the door harder than she'd intended to—her old Honda's doors had to be hauled shut with some force to close completely. "Sorry. I didn't mean to do that. I see you got the scratches taken care of already."

"Friends in high places." He slid his sunglasses down to cover his eyes. "You ready to go for a joyride?"

She forced a smile. "I'd be a fool to say no to a little joy, wouldn't I?"

Adrian drove aimlessly, Sunday driving on a Wednesday afternoon. Whenever someone got behind them, he pulled over to let them pass. "Wonder what's down this road?" he'd say, turning down one potholed track after another.

"Ooh, look at that," she said, pointing out a modern farmhouse perched atop a gentle rise. "How pretty."

"I claim that tractor," he said, referring to the big John Deere some guy was driving across a quaint wooden bridge spanning a winding stream at the foot of the hill.

"What on earth would you do with a tractor?" Heather lifted her face to the breeze as the convertible zoomed around a curve, leaving the farmhouse and tractor behind. "Do you even know how to drive one?"

"I know how to do a lot of things." He gave her a comical leer. "You want me to show you a few of them?"

She smiled, feeling...well...maybe a tiny hint of joy. "Maybe one of these days."

Realizing that he couldn't drive aimlessly forever, Adrian turned back toward the main drag, a narrow backcountry blacktop that wound around the bay. Sometimes the bay was visible; other times they passed long stretches of woodland interspersed with fancy pillared gates that guarded some of the more expensive waterfront estates. He thought he knew where he was going, unless he'd turned the wrong way onto Bayview Drive.

But no, here it was. He slowed just in time to ease into the gravel parking lot of Big Daddy's Bar & Grill. He parked under a cypress tree festooned with Spanish moss and hoped for the best; there were no out-in-the-open spots available. He folded his sunglasses and put them in the console. "Fancy a drink?"

A dozen different excuses flitted across her face before she smiled and said, "Sure. Why not?"

She undid her seat belt and reached for the door handle, but he put a hand on her thigh, a silent cue for her to stay put so he could do the gentlemanly thing and open her door. She nodded and settled for wrapping the long strap around her tiny pink leather purse.

He suspected the tiny purse revealed something about

her. She didn't carry around a bunch of cosmetics and beauty implements or a day-runner and iPad to keep abreast of her important and ever-evolving business concerns or a ton of other unnecessary minutia. He wasn't sure what that revelation meant about her personality, but he decided he was interested in finding out. Could it be that she was one of those rare people who had the ability to inhabit each moment as it came without obsessing over appearances, thinking ahead to the next thing, or planning for every eventuality?

He opened her door and held out a hand to assist her out of the car. She rose gracefully, looking down until the last second when he didn't immediately release her hand. Her eyes met his, a look of hesitant anticipation in those clear, leaf-green depths.

He thought about kissing her. This time, he hoped she wouldn't freeze in dismay. This time, she might even lean into him. He looked at her soft, prettily curved lips, then back up to meet her eyes. He lowered his eyelids in that way that always made her blush. And blush she did, but she also smiled, a tiny secret smile. "Are you going to buy me that drink or what?"

Chapter 4

FRIDAY EVENING, ERIN CAME INTO THE KITCHEN WITH HER backpack slung over one shoulder. She'd gone home with Sierra after school that day and had been dropped off in time for dinner as instructed. "I'm so glad it's the weekend."

"I know. TGIF, right?" Heather gave the pot of noodles she was tending another stir. She'd taken the twins to the shelter after school, and they'd only just gotten home a half hour ago. Spaghetti night had turned into shrimp Alfredo night because frozen shrimp thawed faster than ground beef. "How was the yearbook meeting?"

"Fine. We all got digital cameras on loan from the school, but honestly, I think I'll just use my cell phone." Erin took a clean glass down from the cupboard and filled it with water from the fridge. "I'm gonna head upstairs and do my homework now so I can rest and relax for the rest of the weekend."

"Good plan."

Erin headed toward the stairs.

"Wait up," Heather said. "You fed Charlie before you came in, right?"

"Jeez, Mom." Erin dropped her backpack on the floor and set her water glass on the counter with more force than necessary. "Why do you always jump on me the minute I walk in the door? Why are you punishing me?"

Heather swallowed a sudden surge of temper. "It's not punishment to take care of Charlie. He is your responsibility, and I shouldn't need to remind you that he's the reason you get such a generous allowance. The twins take care of Jasper, you take care of Charlie, and I take care of you kids."

Instead of replying, Erin sent a daggered glance that Heather didn't have to turn around to see because she could feel it boring into the back of her head.

"We all have to help each other," Heather reminded her daughter, as if that would help.

But of course, it only poured oil onto the fire. Erin made a hissing noise that was eerily similar to the one Dale used to make whenever things didn't go his way. "Why don't we just sell Charlie? We might as well, since you won't let me ride him without Daddy here to teach me. He just stands out there in the field, all alone, all day long. It makes me sad."

"I know." Heather blinked back tears. "It makes me sad too. But that horse—"

"The horse you're too scared to even go near," Erin spat.

"Yes. But the horse I'm too scared of…was Dale's horse. And I'm sorry, for Charlie and for you and for me, that I'm just not ready to let him go." She'd thought of it, even gone so far as to contact an equine rescue group. But in the end, she couldn't go through with putting Charlie up for adoption. "Seeing Charlie all alone in that field is sad, but not seeing him at all would be sadder still. So I'm trusting you to take care of him. Maybe we can find someone to teach you how to ride next summer."

"It doesn't make sense!" Erin yelled. "Why are you hanging on to a horse you're too afraid to even touch?"

"Because letting Charlie go would be like letting your dad go all over again, and I'm just not ready to do that."

Erin slumped with a sigh. "Fine. I'll go feed Charlie."

Heather drained and rinsed the noodles, then melted a big chunk of butter over low heat. She poured heavy whipping cream into a jar, dumped in a tablespoon of plain flour, closed the lid, and shook the jar vigorously. The thought of throwing the jar across the room crossed her mind, but she carefully opened the lid and poured the frothy mixture into the saucepan, then stirred in a container of shredded Parmesan cheese. While the sauce thickened, she sautéed the thawed shrimp in a small skillet.

Erin slammed into the kitchen in a huff. "Well, I tried to feed Charlie. I set up his stall, but he wouldn't come. He's just standing out in the field with his head down."

A feeling of dread crept over Heather. "Did you call him?"

Erin made a huff of irritation. "Of course I did. He just stood there."

Heather glanced at the clock. It would be getting dark soon. "Go out there right now, put a halter on him, and make him come in."

Erin groaned. "Why don't *you* do it?"

Heather held on to her temper by the barest tendril of a fraying thread. "I am cooking your dinner, that's why. Look, Erin, I know that you help out more than a lot of kids your age. But this is our life now, whether we like it or not. We all have to pitch in and help each other."

Erin's ice-blue eyes—Dale's eyes—grew sharp as glass, and her mouth drew into a lemon-sucking pucker. After a moment of tight-lipped silence and staring, she stomped her foot. "Fine." She flounced out the back door, slamming it behind her.

Heather went back to stirring the pasta. Her hands trembled, from the argument as much as a sweat-producing fear that something might be wrong with Charlie. The Alfredo sauce was done, so she turned off the heat. The shrimp had curled up and turned pink, so she moved them off the heat and turned that burner off too.

Closing her eyes, she coached herself to take a few deep breaths. Willed her hands to stop shaking. Released tension on a sigh and settled her shoulders, which had crept up to her ears while she'd been arguing with Erin.

They had been such a happy family before.

———————

Cat watched Adrian—whose name he'd figured out by listening to the people who talked to him—from the safe distance of the bushes outside the fence. The other people had finally left, and Cat wondered if Adrian would leave now too. But he sat in the chair and set the flat thing with the hinged lid on the table, then opened it up and started tapping on it as usual.

Humans seemed to be interested in the strangest things.

The flat thing made noises every now and then, but other than that, it seemed to have no use whatsoever. And yet Adrian had an endless capability to stare at the thing and tap on it for great swathes of time.

Enough of that, Cat decided. He came closer and rubbed against the fence, enticing Adrian to come closer so they could study each other with the safety of the fence between them.

Adrian didn't notice.

Cat meowed, arched his back, and paced in the other direction, leaning against the fence.

Adrian threw another of those tasty but rich treats through the fence. Cat had eaten the first two but ignored the rest. He'd eaten too many of those a few days before, and though they tasted better than anything, they gave him the squirts. He'd learned his lesson about those things.

He didn't blame Adrian, though. He knew, without knowing how he knew, that Adrian was a good person who didn't wish him harm. He was also beginning to like that colorful lady who moved like a tree blowing in the wind. She'd been giving him a container of predigested meat every evening. He had to jump the fence and then venture into an open box to get it, but so far, no harm had come to him. Apparently, it wasn't a trap.

Adrian closed the flat thing and stood, stretching. Cat thought at first that the man would come closer, maybe pet Cat through the fence. Cat meowed, a sweet meow of invitation, but Adrian folded the chair, then the table, and leaned them against the fence.

Then Cat heard the low, menacing moan of the big gray tomcat. The one who'd beaten Cat before but didn't seem satisfied with his victory. His wavering yowls meant he was coming to chase Cat away from the predigested food that was his by rights. Cat put his ears back and screamed at the interloper. That was *his* predigested food.

Old Gray could have the treats. Adrian had thrown dozens of them through the fence, and they were incredibly delicious, guaranteed to keep Old Gray busy while Cat scarfed down the gooey meat the tree lady had left for him. Cat could eat his food and abscond before Old Gray found and ate all those scattered treats.

All he had to do was stay out of sight until Old Gray got the squirts. Then the old tomcat wouldn't feel like chasing Cat again for a good long time. But Cat realized that sooner or later, he would have to choose between freedom and safety.

Heather called the twins down to dinner. She had just set their plates in front of them at the kitchen bar when Erin slammed through the back door.

"Mom." Erin's eyes were wide with panic; her breaths came in frantic huffs. "Charlie's lying down in the field. He won't get up."

A frisson of fear skittered up Heather's spine. "He... He won't get up?" She'd heard Erin but hoped she had misunderstood somehow. She didn't know a lot about horses. But she did understand enough to know that a lying-down horse who wouldn't get up was a serious problem.

Josh and Caroline had stopped eating, forks suspended in midair. They both spoke at once. "What's wrong with Charlie?"

Heather put a hand up to shush them and turned back to Erin. "You tried to put a halter on him?"

Erin nodded. "I got it on him, but he didn't even pick up his head."

Heather chewed on a fingernail. The vet's office was already closed. She could call the office and leave a message, but it would take as much as an hour for Mack to call her back.

"Mom," Erin said in a pleading tone, "I think Charlie is really sick. We need to do something."

"I know that," Heather snapped. Then she put a hand on Erin's shoulder. "I'm sorry. I'm thinking about what to do."

The kids were all staring at her, waiting for her to make a decision. "I'll handle this," she told them. "Y'all finish your dinner."

She took her cell phone into the den. Reva probably had Mack's cell number. Maybe she could get in touch with him right away. She sat on the couch and called her friend. Relief flowed through her when Reva picked up immediately. "Hey, you."

Heather didn't waste time on pleasantries. "Charlie is lying down in the field, and he won't get up. Do you have Mack's cell number?"

"I do. I'll call him for you and then head that way myself. If Charlie is already down, it may take us all working together to get him up again."

"Oh, thank you, thank you." Having Reva's support made this whole situation seem a little less dire. "What should I be doing for him while I wait?"

"First priority is to get him standing. What you don't want is for him to roll over because he could twist his intestines, and then you'd be talking about surgery."

"I'll try." But she couldn't imagine herself having any

success at moving Charlie from five feet away. She knew her phobia of horses wasn't logical, but that didn't lessen her fear.

"Get Jasper to help. But if you can't get Charlie up, at least try to keep him from rolling. I'll call Mack and head your way. See you soon."

When Heather ended the call, she noticed Erin hovering in the archway between the kitchen and the den. "What now?"

Heather tucked the phone into the back pocket of her jeans. "Reva says that if we can't get Charlie up, we at least need to keep him lying still. If he rolls over, it could hurt his insides."

"I'll go out there and sit by him," Erin said. "If I hold his head still, he won't be able to roll."

A vision of the horse kicking out at Erin or rolling over her invaded Heather's mind.

"He won't hurt me." Erin had correctly read Heather's expression, a feat Heather knew wasn't difficult because every fleeting emotion showed on her face. "I'll be sitting next to his head," Erin added, "not by his feet."

"I understand that, honey. I just worry."

Erin gave Heather a quick hug. "I know; you're a mom. Worrying is your job."

Heather kissed Erin's cheek. "Let's do this."

Erin called Jasper and headed that way. Heather paused in the kitchen to give the twins instructions to stay inside and watch something on TV until Erin came back in to supervise bath time and tuck them into bed. Then, with her heart thumping against the lump in her throat, she hurried to catch up.

———————

Charlie felt the cool, damp earth beneath him, seeping into his body and cooling the pain in his belly. But the griping pains didn't stop. They built and then eased, built and then eased, never completely going away, always coming back stronger than before. He closed his eyes and ground his teeth against the pain.

Something he couldn't understand kept him tethered to the earth. Tethered to the pain. Tethered to the people who didn't understand him or care about him or have time for him. Why? Was it because he hadn't yet suffered enough to make up for his failures? Was it because he had to be punished for his sins?

He was willing to be punished. He knew he deserved it. So he closed his eyes and kept his focus on the twisting pain in his belly. He let the pain come. He didn't turn away from it, and he didn't want to. Because he deserved it. It belonged to him. It was all he had left.

Moments later, he felt Erin's gentle touch on his face. Then Charlie felt Heather's hands on him too. She smoothed back the mane along his neck, and Charlie shivered as the warm evening breeze reached his sweat-damp skin.

"Mom," Erin said. "I can't believe you're sitting this close to Charlie."

"Neither can I." Heather's voice sounded as soft as her touch felt. "But he's a little less scary when he isn't standing upright."

"I hope he's gonna be okay." Erin's voice wobbled. "I'm so scared for him."

"Me too, honey," Heather said. "Me too."

Jasper whined, nosing at Charlie's face. Charlie tried to lift his head to greet his old friend, but even that small movement seemed impossible.

"Reva said that maybe Jasper could help us get Charlie up," Heather said. "Let's try it."

Erin tugged at Charlie's halter, and Heather tried to lift his neck, while Jasper barked in Charlie's ears, a ringing, annoying repetition of "Get up, get up, get up."

Charlie pedaled his feet weakly, but it was no use. He couldn't get his feet under him now, even if he wanted to.

Author's Note

I love, love, love hearing from my readers! You can catch me on my website (contact us page), on Facebook (personal and author pages), or email me at ccbrown66@att.net.

I try to answer all my mail personally but sometimes if I'm working on a deadline, it may be a couple of days. Without readers, authors would soon top the list of extinct species, so please know that you are appreciated.

Please also take the time to share your thoughts on this book with other readers on Amazon or Goodreads.